THE DEMON IN THE SNOW

A movement to Kit's right made him spin around. His eyes probed the shadows and saw nothing. Was his brain playing tricks on him? A flicker of movement deep in the forest caught his eye. Kit went rigid and his heart leaped to his throat. Skimming across the snow was something—something like the shape of a woman—or so he thought at first. Her long hair was fluttering in the wind behind her, and her clothes seemed to drift up as if buoyed by some unseen hand.

But it could not have been a woman, or a man, for it moved too swiftly across the deep snow. Kit blinked to make sure. The shock of seeing the apparition held him there. It wasn't a woman, couldn't be a woman! Even though the distance was great, nearly at the edge of his vision, he was certain that although the creature, whatever it was, was running on two legs like a human, it had upon its head a rack of antlers like that of a deer or elk!

KIT CARSON

MOUNTAIN DEMON

DOUG HAWKINS

LEISURE BOOKS NEW YORK CITY

A LEISURE BOOK®

October 1999

Published by

Dorchester Publishing Co., Inc.
276 Fifth Avenue
New York, NY 10001

ISBN 0-8439-4619-9

ACKNOWLEDGMENTS

My sincerest thanks to the late Dr. Thomas Edward, who so graciously allowed me to roam freely through his rare and valuable collection of monographs by that nineteenth-century Native American scholar, Professor W. G. F. Smith.

MOUNTAIN DEMON

Chapter One

"Aye, and I still say it's damned peculiar, a grown man carrying around that doll with him like he does," Sean O'Farrell scoffed in his thick, Irish brogue. With the words came a cloud of frozen breath that hung momentarily in the frigid air past his icicle-fringed fiery red beard, dissipating finally against the upturned collar of his shaggy buffalo coat. "And don't go telling me I'm to blame for him running off like he did!"

The four men rode single file. No one spoke for a moment, each huddled deep inside heavy coats as their horses broke a fresh trail through the endless white that had descended upon the mountains. Except for the men's constant low bickering, the crunch of frozen snow beneath their horses' hooves, the sounds of small avalanches from overburdened pine boughs, or the occasional pop of freezing tree sap, the mountain-side was drenched in a deep, eerie silence.

Today was the first break they had had in a storm that had raged for over a week. The first opportunity for the men to mount a search for one of their own, Andy Bodine, missing three days now. To Kit Carson, riding at the head of the column, the intensity of the quiet seemed out of place for such a bright, cloudless day.

The field of snow stretching away across the valley was blindingly bright. He looked away, peering into the forest that climbed the mountainside at his left, to keep his eyes from hurting.

Three years earlier Kit, Jim Bridger, Gray Feather, and Mark Head had spent a month of trapping not very far from here, living in a makeshift cabin. Three years earlier they had a passel of Blackfeet warriors to contend with. This year no trapper had seen hide nor hair of Bug's Boys. It was smallpox. The disease had driven the Indians north, leaving a trail of dead men and women in their hasty retreat to put the white man's death far behind them.

"You didn't need to ride him about it like you done," Thomas Conner said after a few minutes, breaking the long, uncomfortable silence. He looked at O'Farrell with hard eyes, narrowing in the snow glare beneath eyebrows frosted with ice crystals. Conner was a young man, feeling out his first winter in the mountains. He and Andy Bodine had hit it off right at at the start, and he was feeling particularly bitter toward this man who had started the trouble. Conner was leading a fifth horse—Bodine's horse. It had returned to the winter encampment riderless less than a day after Bodine had left.

"Bodine is a big boy," O'Farrell shot back.

"Even big boys hurt when you strike at their under-belly," Gray Feather noted. Waldo Gray Feather Smith was the philosopher among them. Half Ute Indian and half white, he had spent the first twelve years of his life among his mother's people, with the tribe of Chief Walkara. The second twelve he spent with his white father, who had built a small fortune in a shipping concern on the Erie Canal. Horace Smith had seen to it that Waldo got a brilliant education at Harvard College. But the mountains and his mother's people were a siren's call he could not resist, and Gray Feather returned with the notion that he could teach the Utes to read, write, and speak proper English. Walkara, however, had other ideas. The stubborn chief fervently believed that the language soon to overtake the Rocky Mountains would be Spanish, not English. That was about the time Gray Feather met Kit Carson, and he and Kit had been riding the trapper's trail ever since.

O'Farrell looked over his shoulder at Gray Feather, who rode between him and Connor, and said, "Him being a grown man, Mr. Feather, he ought not be playing with wee dolls."

"Maybe he has a reason for having it," Gray Feather answered reasonably. "Something that is none of your business."

O'Farrell scowled at the Indian. "Now, just you be telling me, what sort of reason might that be?"

Gray Feather shrugged. "I don't know. But it neither picked your pockets nor broke your bones . . . and it wasn't your place to call him down on it."

"You be minding that tongue, Mr. Feather, or—"

"All right, you two!" Kit Carson drew rein and

turned his horse to face O'Farrell and Gray Feather. Conner and the extra horse came to a halt behind him. Kit had been listening to them bickering ever since they had rode away from their winter quarters on the Powder River earlier that morning. He speared O'Farrell with a narrowed eye. "I'm getting mighty tired of the three of you casting blame about. Bodine is out here someplace and lost. For all we know, he might be dead. Instead of wasting time arguing about whose fault it was that he rode off, you ought to be keeping your eyes peeled and ears open. If he's still alive and hurt, he might be trying to signal us. The way you're carrying on, we could ride right past him and never hear." Kit nodded at the extra horse that Conner was leading. "We know that Bodine is afoot, and that's a bad way to be this time of the year and with this storm."

A pile of gray clouds was beginning to bank up against the western sky. "This break in the weather won't last long. Let's make the best of it while we're able." Kit yanked his horse's head about and urged the animal on.

They rode on, searching for signs of the lost man upon the vast, unbroken blanket of snow that whitened the mountains. The sun glare made looking across it nearly impossible, and blasts of icy wind stung their cheeks and bit savagely through their buffalo-skin coats.

The break did not last, and shortly the storm rolled in again. Buckskin gloves and badger-skin hats offered little protection against the plunging temperatures when the sky began to cloud over. The only good

Kit could see in the weeklong storm rearing its head once more was that the clouds cut off the sun's brilliance, allowing them to peer hard and searchingly across the snow fields.

As he rode through the cold, head pulled down into his thick coat collar like a turtle's, Kit's thoughts went back to the beginning, to how it had all started. He had lost track of how many times he had revisited that single incident, but whenever he did, he knew that he was as much to blame for Bodine leaving the protection of winter quarters as anyone else there. But there was no doubt that it had been O'Farrell's thoughtless remark that had set the calamity in motion.

"What is that you have there, Mr. Bodine?" had been an innocent enough question. But O'Farrell had not really cared what it was. He was only looking for something to take his mind off the long weeks of confinement. Off the howling winds that buffeted the five cabins on the Powder River where nearly two dozen trappers had been holed up for the last eight weeks. Christmas had come and gone with hardly anyone taking notice, and it was already well into January.

Winter quarter affected men differently. Some took to it stoically and philosophically, seeing it as just another trial to be endured, or an opportunity to take advantage of. Gray Feather, for instance, was happy as a jay in a raspberry patch just to pore over his thick tome of Shakespeare. Kit, like many of the others, used the time to make and repair clothes, clean and oil rifles and pistols, or shape bullets from the soft lead bars they had traded for at the summer rendezvous.

O'Farrell, on the other hand, seemed to care little

for any of that. He had been growing more and more impatient with the storm that showed no signs of letting up. Kit had seen it coming. O'Farrell was a man in desperate need of diversion—any diversion. Bodine's misfortune in revealing the Indian maiden doll with the long black hair and cross-stitched eyes and mouth had been just what the surly Irishman had been looking for.

"It's nothing," Bodine said, quickly tucking the doll back into his hunting bag, out of sight. Andy Bodine was a slight-built man of twenty-nine with a long, slender nose and bright, blue eyes. He had lost his hair early on—always a plus in a land where a thick thatch would likely catch the eye of every red buck with a scalping knife. Bodine had no fears in that department. His ability to grow hair had migrated from his head to his chin, where a robust auburn beard was the envy of every man there—especially during this cold season.

"Nothing, my ass." O'Farrell rose from the side of the fire pit and stood over the trapper. "Let me see it."

There was a sudden electricity in the air.

Gray Feather set his book upon his lap, marking his place with a finger. Kit ceased drawing his butcher knife across the whetstone and looked over. Thomas Conner had been writing a letter—one of those neverending pieces that someday would be put into the hands of a trader heading back east with the hope of it eventually finding its way to the person for whom it had been written. He put down his pen.

"I said it was nothing, O'Farrell." Bodine closed the flap and started to button it.

O'Farrell snatched the hunting bag away from him. Bodine made a grab for it, but O'Farrell backed out of his reach, grinning. He had the bag opened and the little doll out, hooting in delight, showing it to everyone there by the time Bodine could get to his feet.

"A big grown-up fellow like yourself, playing with dolls?"

"Give it to me!"

O'Farrell laughed and shuffled it back and forth, just out of Bodine's reach. Having longer arms, O'Farrell managed to keep it from the other man. This way and that they went, one reaching, one dodging. For a moment it appeared the two of them were dancing in the middle of the cabin.

"O'Farrell," Kit said finally. "Give it back to him."

The Irishman laughed, hooting, "Let's see if Mr. Bodine can take it back from me." Then, ducking his head, O'Farrell leaped over the low fire, thrust his hand up through the smoke hole in the roof, and pretended to fling the doll outside. But using a bit of sleight of hand he quickly tucked it under his belt in the small of his back instead.

"I don't have it anymore," he said, holding out both hands.

Kit had seen what he had done.

Bodine scowled at the grinning Irishman and started for the door.

"O'Farrell!" Kit barked, losing patience with the man's foolishness. "Give it back to him now!"

Bodine wheeled about as the doll reappeared in O'Farrell's hands. "I have me a wee niece back in County Cork who plays with dolls, Mr. Bodine," he teased. "But she's a lass, and lasses play with dolls. Why do you do it?"

Bodine had taken about all that he was going to. Kit saw it coming and reckoned O'Farrell deserved whatever Bodine could dish out. But the cramped confines of the tiny cabin was no place for a fight.

Thomas Conner set his pen and paper aside, grabbed up a stout piece of firewood, and readied himself just in case his friend had trouble with the bigger man.

"O'Farrell," Kit said again, standing now. "You've carried this far enough. Give the doll back to him."

"I'm just starting to have me some fun, Mr. Carson." O'Farrell dangled the doll by its hair and held it out over the fire.

Bodine seemed to snap right then. His eyes went wild and he grabbed for a tomahawk lying nearby.

Kit sprang and caught Bodine's arm as the sharp ax was swinging out. He deflected it just in time, while a suddenly dumbfounded and startled O'Farrell could only stand there staring. Kit wrestled the weapon from Bodine's fist and shoved him back against the wall.

"Enough of this! O'Farrell, give me the doll!" Kit demanded.

Without any further argument, Sean O'Farrell put the small figure in Kit's outstretched hand. Kit turned an angry eye on Bodine. "I know that O'Farrell can be a bother and a pain when he gets like this, but killing weapons have no place in your disagreement with him. If you two want to bloody each other's noses, take this fight outside and have at it. But leave the weapons inside!" Kit shoved the doll into Bodine's fist and backed away from him, wary of what the man might do next.

What Bodine *did* do next was completely unexpected. Without a word he shoved the doll back inside his hunting bag, pulled on his heavy buffalo-skin coat, and, grabbing up pistols and rifle, he left. The door hung open for a few seconds, letting the icy wind and swirling snow fill the cabin and fan the flames of their fire. The men looked at each other, no one speaking. Kit went outside. Bodine was trudging through the snow toward the lean-to near the corral. He grabbed up a saddle and blanket and ducked under the poles of their crude corral. Through the driving snow Kit watched him toss the saddle onto his horse. It was too cold to just stand there in his shirtsleeves, and Kit returned to the cabin.

"What's he doing?" Conner asked worriedly.

Kit frowned and shrugged into his coat. "Looks like he needs to ride his anger out some."

"In this weather?" Gray Feather said, inserting a more permanent bookmark and rising.

"I'll go talk to him." Kit yanked his badger-skin hat onto his head.

"Maybe I ought to go with you," Conner offered.

Kit knew the two men were close friends. Conner just might be able to talk some sense into the angry trapper. "All right."

"Maybe I should go too," O'Farrell said with a note of contriteness in his voice.

"No, you've already done enough damage," Kit answered. "You just stay here."

Just then they heard the pounding of hooves. Kit and

Thomas hurried outside in time to see Andy Bodine riding down toward the river. Bodine crossed over on the thick ice and turned his animal toward the north, where he was quickly lost to sight beyond a veil of driven snow.

From the other cabins half a dozen men ventured out into the cold to see what the commotion was all about. Looking stern in his big coat, Jim Bridger high-stepped his way through the deep snow.

"What happened?"

Kit frowned. "Bodine and O'Farrell got into a scrap. I came down pretty hard on Bodine for losing his temper, and he took off."

"Took off? Off to where?" Bridger squinted hard into the blowing snow, but it was impossible to see farther than a hundred yards.

"I don't know, Gabe. Reckon he just needed to ride off some of that steam. He'll be back."

"Hope so." Bridger did not sound convinced, and the men returned to their cabins.

That had been three days earlier.

Bodine never did come back, but his horse did about twelve hours later.

O'Farrell's words intruded on Kit's reverie, pulling his thoughts back to the present. "Saints preserve me, it's cold," he proclaimed, beating his arms about himself. He glanced to the darkening sky as the first of the returning snow began to fall. A wind picked up, driving the cold farther into their shivering bones. "This is hopeless!"

It *was* cold. Deadly cold. "Like a grave" was an appropriate description, especially for a man alone, afoot, and possibly injured. Kit was built along the same lines as Bodine. A slight, wiry man, he was more hard muscle than soft fat; cat quick and tough as an old maple tree. But cold weather and icy winds cut through him like a Comanche war lance. It was days like this that made him think longingly of Taos. Down in New Mexico winters were always pleasant, with little snow and an abundance of warm, sunny days. A perfect place for a man to build a home and put down roots. Someday, he promised himself, someday he would buy himself a little house there, perhaps near his good friend Charles Bent. He'd bring his new Arapaho wife, Waa-nibe, down from the mountains and start a family. Someday, he thought wistfully, someday . . .

"Mr. Carson," O'Farrell bellowed. "How long are we going to keep at this? There ain't no tracks to follow, and we've not come across a single sign that Mr. Bodine has been through here at all. Saints! We keep this up much longer and the old woman from the fairy mound will begin to wail for us! I say we turn back and make for the encampment before we end up like Mr. Bodine. Mark my words, we'll not be finding that poor fellow till spring comes back and melts off all this snow and ice!"

Kit reined around to face them. The cold was starting to get to them, although neither Gray Feather nor Conner seemed ready to give up the search just yet. As much as Kit wanted to deny it, Sean O'Farrell was right. They had been looking for hours. The storm had erased any tracks Bodine might have left behind. It was useless to search further, and with another storm moving in, it could be deadly. Kit knew of a cabin nearby where they could hole up until this new threat passed them, but what good would waiting until later do? If they had not found any signs of Bodine by now, they never would—especially after a second storm dumped another two feet of snow on these mountains.

"I say we keep looking," Conner said.

Gray Feather was frowning when Kit shifted his view toward the Ute.

"And what do you say?" Kit respected the Indian's opinion. Although Gray Feather had spent half his life living in the East, he had a certain innate knowledge of these things—a knowledge that comes with having been born in the mountains.

"I want to find him as bad as you do, but common sense tells me we're just running around in circles out here." Gray Feather glanced at the angry skies. "If this one is as bad as the last, we'd best make for cover soon."

Kit nodded. "That's about the way I see it, too. All right. We go back."

"We can't!" Conner said. "Andy's out here someplace. We can't leave him!"

"And we can't find him, either," O'Farrell interjected.

"You never wanted to find Andy," Conner shot back. "You only came along to save face. Because it was all your doing that he's out here in the first place!"

"That ain't true! I want to find him like everyone else. But I don't want to freeze to death trying."

"We don't need this squabbling now," Kit said, breaking off their angry words. "We're heading back, Conner, and that's all there is to it."

Kit clucked and urged his horse back the way they had come, hoping to beat the storm to their cabin on the Powder.

He had gone only a couple dozen steps when the report of a pistol shot rolling down the mountainside brought him to a stop.

"It's Bodine!" Conner declared, wheeling his horse around as he scanned the trees. "It's gotta be!"

"Only one way to find out." Kit turned his horse in the direction of the report and kicked her into motion.

Chapter Two

The deep snow hampered their attempt to climb the steep terrain. Puffing like steam engines, the horses scrambled and clawed at it, in some places sinking nearly to their cinch buckles in the dry, powdery stuff. Finally Kit brought the riders to a halt and cocked an ear. The frozen land around them was as silent as a graveyard at midnight. He called out Bodine's name, then waited. The men glanced at each other, the expectancy on their faces slowly fading.

"He can't hear you," Conner said, hope sinking.

Then a second shot rang out, closer this time and a little to their left.

"Over thar!" The horses plowed through the knee-high snow. Kit called out to Bodine again. Coming in among a field of scattered rocks, only their tips showing above the snow, Kit spied a scrap of buffalo fur poking out from behind one of them, half buried in the snow.

They sprang from their saddles and plowed through the deep drifts. In the lee of the rock, on a patch of ground swept free of the snow by the wind, lay Andy Bodine. Against the rock was the remains of a fire that had burned itself out some time before.

"Andy!" Conner cried, breaking his way through the last few feet of drifts and dropping to his knees beside his friend.

Bodine blinked and looked around as if in a daze as Conner elevated his head onto his knees. "Andy, you're gonna be all right now."

"Tom?" Bodine's eyes seemed to be having trouble focusing. "Kit? Is that you?" He gave a short laugh and groaned, "So, I wasn't dreaming it after all."

Kit hunkered down beside the man, placing a hand upon the woolly coat. "You gave us a big worry, Andy. Thought we'd be finding you in the spring once all this snow melted. You hurt bad?"

"Damn horse took a spill and gave me a tumble, he did. A good one. Hit hard. Busted up my leg."

Kit glanced around at the rocks that cut the wind. "Least you were able to made it to cover."

"I did that, all right. Crawled a couple hundred yards from where the damned animal threw me. Found this place where the snow didn't gather. Had me a nice fire until I run out of wood. Crawled around some to collect more, but snow come down so hard it buried most of it. Wind kept this little place free, only to pile it up right deep on my busted leg till I couldn't

23

move no more. I hurt like the devil for a while, then the pain sort of went away. But by then I was too weak to do anything about it."

"Whal, we'll get you to shelter and have a look at that leg, Andy."

A violent shiver shook him. "All . . . all I want is a fire to warm myself by and something hot to drink."

Kit saw the spent pistol at the man's side, and a second one still clutched in his fingers. "Good thing you managed to see us down below and give out a signal. We'd have never found you tucked away up here amongst these boulders."

In spite of his feeble condition, Bodine managed a small laugh. "See you? Hell, I didn't *see* you, Kit. It was that loudmouth Irishman. I could hear him blustering all the way up here. Good thing Bug's Boys ain't about. He'd have called them all down on you."

O'Farrell gave a lame grin. "See here, if it wasn't for my *blustering*, you would have ended up freezing to death back here."

"If it wasn't for you, Andy wouldn't have been here in the first place," Conner retorted.

"You two stop riding each other," Kit ordered. He looked at Gray Feather. "Remember that cabin we built someplace around here a while back?"

"I remember it. Spent a whole year there with you, Bridger, and Head."

"A year? It was only a few weeks."

Gray Feather made a wry grin. "Well, it sure seemed like a year."

Kit frowned. "I don't need it from you too. Think you can find it again?"

24

"I think so, if I wanted to."

"Better leave now, before this weather gets much worse. Take O'Farrell with you. Make the place fit to live as best you can. Me and Conner will bring Bodine along directly."

"Why not just head back to winter quarters?" O'Farrell asked.

"Too far. We'd never make it now with this storm closing in on us and Bodine in such a bad way."

Gray Feather said, "If I remember right, we're not more than a mile from the cabin. It should still be standing." He stuck a foot into his stirrup and swung up onto the horse. "We'll be waiting for you, Kit."

O'Farrell climbed back onto his horse and looked down at Bodine. He frowned and seemed to want to say something. But he didn't. He turned away, following Gray Feather down into the valley below.

"Think you can fork a horse, Andy?" Kit asked when they had left.

"If you two can get me in the saddle, I can ride."

"Sure you can, Andy. You'll do fine. It'll just be a matter of holding on tight," Conner encouraged as he and Kit picked Bodine up off the ground. They brushed the snow from him and eased him onto his horse. Gritting back the pain, Bodine grabbed the horn in both hands and leaned forward until his bushy, icicle-fringed beard nearly touched the animal's neck. Kit went back for the pistols, and after hunting around a bit asked Bodine where his rifle was.

"Lost it in the snow when I got thrown."

"Too bad. It'll be hard to replace."

"Not as hard as this child's hide if you boys hadn't showed up. Mighty grateful you did."

"Couldn't leave you out here, you ol' coot," Conner said.

Bodine managed another grin, then closed his eyes, holding on tight.

Kit shoved the pistols into the deep pockets of his coat and swung up onto his horse. They turned into the tracks left by Gray Feather and O'Farrell, moving slowly for Bodine's sake. Kit took the lead, with Conner holding the reins of Bodine's horse.

The storm thickened around them until following the fresh tracks became difficult. Blowing snow stung their cheeks and bit deep into their coats. Bodine was suffering most from the cold, and he was hardly fit to ride. It held them back, and they could move only so fast. Kit hoped that Gray Feather had been able to find the old cabin after three years, and that it had remained livable. The make-do shelter hadn't been much to begin with when they had built it. The chimney had been thrown together with flat, ill-fitting stones, and since it had been summer at the time, the trappers had not bothered to chink them, or the logs. It had been meant only as a temporary refuge. There had not even been a real door, just a scrap of bear skin to cover it, and another for the hole in the wall that had served as a window. But it was the roof that Kit most worried about. Cottonwood bark and pine boughs piled onto cross-poles of green aspen had been all that it was, and he suspected that by now it was all tumbled in on itself.

In the gray half-light of the swirling snow, the men

were but indistinct shapes of wind-whipped shaggy buffalo fur. Conner had tucked his head down into his collar while Bodine was bent forward, clutching the saddle, barely holding on. Kit prayed Gray Feather had found the cabin, and that it was not too far ahead.

Time seemed to stand still as their horses trudged on. Suddenly Kit detected a hint of smoke.

"Thar up ahead!" he shouted back to the men over the roar of the wind.

Five minutes later they came to a clearing in the trees and the half-buried shape of a cabin Kit remembered well. The crude chimney was puffing smoke, and a bit of light from the fire burning inside brightened the window opening. Outside, O'Farrell was chopping away at a pile of fresh-cut pine boughs, fitting them to the low roof. Inside, Gray Feather had constructed a makeshift broom from the same and was busily sweeping out the snow.

The work came to a standstill as they gathered around and helped Bodine out of the saddle. Inside the cabin, they laid him upon a pallet of saddle blankets Gray Feather had already prepared for him. In spite of the howling wind outside, and the openings in the cabin, the fire had raised the temperature enough to take the edge off the cold.

Kit and O'Farrell tackled the roof, putting it back together while Gray Feather and Conner took the horses to a makeshift corral with the others. They stripped off the saddles and bedrolls, and hauled the saddle blankets to the cabin to fashion a cover for the window and door. Afterward, the men gathered what firewood they could find sticking up through the deep snow. Kit remembered that this place had been bountiful in downed wood, but right now most of it was under two or three feet of white drifts, and they were forced to cut green to supplement the dry.

Dusk came early as the blinding snow and low clouds choked the daylight from the land. It was well after dark by the time they had put everything back in order and finally closed the blanket door and set a log upon its end to keep it in place.

The shelter itself was a mix of dugout and log cabin. When they had built it three years before, Kit, Gray Feather, Bridger, and Head had merely dug a pit about eight feet square and three feet deep. It was around this that they had built the cabin whose four-foot walls and shed roof combined gave them barely enough headroom to stand. The fireplace wasn't much more than a circle of boulders with a dozen or so flat slabs of stones arranged to direct smoke up through a hole in the roof. It drew poorly but worked well enough to keep a fire burning. Slowly, the place warmed to a tolerable temperature.

Shedding his heavy coat, Kit turned his attention to Andy Bodine. The injured trapper had been drifting in and out of consciousness the whole time.

"Leg hurt bad?" Kit asked, splitting Bodine's buckskin trousers with his butcher knife.

"Hurts some, below the knee. Must be where it's busted," Bodine answered, his head propped upon one of the saddles, staring at the pine boughs overhead.

"Whal, it appears to have swollen up like a pumpkin. You'll begin to feel it again once we set the thing,

I can promise you that." Kit unlaced the moccasin and stripped it off along with a heavy woolen sock.

O'Farrell remained in the corner tending the fire as Conner and Gray Feather crowded over Kit's shoulder for a look.

Bodine folded an arm across his eyes and gave a short laugh. "You let me know when you're about to set it, Kit. I want to be ready for it."

Kit grimaced and glanced at Gray Feather. The Ute frowned and gave a slow shake of his head. For a long moment no one spoke.

"Well, let's get it over with," Bodine said.

Conner gave a soft groan, then, shaking his head, he looked away.

"You feel this?" Kit asked, prodding the puffy skin with the point of his knife.

The flesh of Bodine's foot and lower leg was dark red, and now a faint odor had begun to fill the cabin.

"Feel what?"

Kit hoped against hope that he was wrong, but there was no mistaking the early sign.

Bodine sensed the sudden tension that overcame the men and filled the cabin. "What is it? What's wrong?"

"It's a mite worse than just a broken leg, Andy," he said.

Bodine put his arm down and looked at him. "How bad?"

Although he was not a physician, Kit had seen this condition plenty of times . . . and the usual outcome of the affliction. He understood, too, that beating around the bush would not be doing Bodine any favor either.

"You got a frostbite, Andy, and it don't look good."

* * *

They had hung their buffalo-skin coats around the walls of the old cabin, blocking most of the wind and lending a cozy feel to the little shelter. Outside, the blizzard raged, piling snow against the sides and onto the flimsy roof. Although they had taken care to weave the pine boughs together, the ceiling was beginning to sag under the weight. Keeping the snow swept off would be a task that would keep them busy all night.

The odor of brewed coffee helped dispel some of the gloom. They had plenty of jerked venison to eat, and for the time being Bodine was resting comfortably with a full belly and coffee to help warm his insides. Kit had held off setting the broken leg and left the frostbitten limb exposed to the warmth of the fire in the slight chance that it was not as bad as it had first seemed and that perhaps the heat might revive the skin. But he held out no great hope that that would happen.

"Have you ever seen such a storm?" Bodine asked at one point. The men listened a moment to the wind howling through the trees outside and whistling past the cracks in the unchinked log walls.

"It's been many a winter," Kit allowed thoughtfully.

O'Farrell shivered in spite of the warmth of the fire. He peered up at the sagging ceiling. "Listen to her a-wailing, will you. Saints protect us if it don't sound exactly like a banshee's cry."

"Since when have you ever heard a banshee's cry?" Conner scoffed.

O'Farrell's face went stark in the firelight. He stared at Conner with wide, unblinking eyes that reflected the dancing flames. "I have heard her, Mr. Conner. Twice in my life have I heard the cry of the old woman of the fairy mounds."

"When?"

"Both times when I was but a lad. The first was just before my uncle Daniel O'Farrell died. Me and my whole family heard her at that time. Then, three years later, she came again. I was alone when I heard her wailing just outside the window of our house. But when I looked, no one was there. No sound at all except for the flutter of bird's wings flapping away. I knew her for what she was then. She'd come to tell me someone was about to die. Not one week later my father dropped over dead while pitching hay into the loft."

"You heard it for your father and his brother?"

"Heard *her*. A banshee is woman. She's a family spirit, you know. The herald of death, she is."

"A family spirit? What's that?"

"She belongs to a family—stays with that family. And she comes to that family whenever someone is about to die."

Conner gave a laugh, but the foreboding look etched in O'Farrell's face cut it off short.

"She'll follow a family member, wherever he goes to." O'Farrell's fixed gaze seemed to pierce right through Conner, as if he was seeing something else, something in the past, Kit reckoned.

"Even clear across the wide Atlantic if she has too," O'Farrell added softly, ominously.

"That's just myth and fairy tales," Conner declared.

Bodine hitched himself up on his elbows and said, "Well, I've heard some strange tales myself."

Conner glanced over. "What kind of tales?"

"It gives me the shakes to think about it. I don't know that I should speak of it now. It's been years since it happened. I was a lad when I got the story from my father, who actually knew the gent who had the encounter."

"Encounter? What encounter?" O'Farrell's curiosity was piqued, and he leaned forward, eyes intent. "What happened?"

Bodine glanced around the cozy place, his view lingering upon each of them each, and finally shifting about the cabin as if searching for hidden listeners as well. "I don't know if I should be mentioning it . . . "

"Tell us what happened, Andy," Conner urged.

Kit put a burning brand to the bowl of his clay pipe and said around its stem, "I could go for a good yarn about now." It would keep Andy's thoughts from the mortifying leg, and they were all in the mood for some harmless diversion. "Since you've already started, you can't just quit and leave us hanging, Andy." He blew a ring of smoke at the sagging ceiling.

"Well, all right. Suppose it can't hurt, not here anyway, so far from where it all happened." His voice was suddenly low, and strangely wary. "Only, it ain't a yarn, Kit. It's true, everything I'm about to tell you. If we were back home in Kentuck, and anywhere near Injun Hollow, I'd not be speaking a word of it. No one talks of it back home." Again his eyes darted around as if searching for uninvited listeners.

Gray Feather closed his volume of Shakespeare and watched Bodine with intense interest. "Let's hear the story."

"All right, I'll tell it. When I was a kid we had us a neighbor who used to live down below us, in a place called Injun Hollow, about a mile and a half from our farm. His name was Donald MacFadden. MacFadden was fond of tipping back a jug of whiskey now and again, and when he got into his cups, his dalliance became legendary. His poor wife, Hillary, she put up with this embarrassment for years, never speaking a word against her husband, or his wandering ways.

"Well, one Friday MacFadden walked into town with his two dogs, Clarence and Toby, at his heels. He was on an errand to collect a new pair of boots from the cobbler, which he did. Before starting back home, since daylight was still in the sky, MacFadden took a detour by way of the Saddle and Bit public house for a pint of swamp root, a pipe or two of tobacco, and some pleasant camaraderie with the mayor and the farrier, who happened to be there. As was the pattern of things where Donald MacFadden was concerned, one pint led to two, and two to three, and the respite that was only to be a stopover of an hour or two lasted late into the night. The barkeeper finally booted him out, and the mayor and farrier sent Donald on his way home sometime after midnight.

"Now, the road into Injun Hollow can be a long, lonely place after the witching hour has come and gone. At one point it dips down past a swampy place where the vapors rise and scud about, drifting across the lane. Balls of light have been known to rise up suddenly and dance upon the still waters."

Bodine paused, staring at the trappers. He had their attention, all right, and he lowered his voice, speaking softly and as if to keep from being overheard. "Men have been known to disappear in that swamp without a trace. No one walks that road after dark, and *never* alone if they have a lick of sense in their heads.

"MacFadden was too drunk to care right then, so away he went, bold as brass, taking the lane deep into the swampy place, his two dogs trotting along at his side. Suddenly up ahead he sees something standing among the vapors, by the water's edge. It's the figure of a person, or so he judges, but it's not moving. Pale in color it was, dressed in a long gown, wearing a wide bonnet. Donald stops, his breath catching. He squints hard to be sure, and wonders if maybe it ain't only the stump of a tree, laced in the swirling mist, tricking his eyes. But then it turns slowly toward him. MacFadden can't see the face, because the bonnet hides that, but he knows it's the figure of a woman, tall and slender, with a basket over her arm.

"Clarence and Toby, they begin to whimper, and tuck their tails, shying back some. But Donald, he's intrigued, and being drunk, throws caution to the wind. Recovering from his surprise at seeing the woman standing there, he fixes a cocksure grin upon his sodden face and starts ahead. The dogs stop and refuse to go another step. He tries to make them come, but they balk, turn tail, and make tracks away from there."

"What was it they feared?" O'Farrell asked nervously.

Bodine fixed him with wide, unblinking eyes and went on with his story. "Donald MacFadden walked up to her, and in the dark saw that she cut a fine figure of a woman, although he can't see her face. 'What are you doing in a place like this, at this hour, all alone?' he asks. 'I'm on my way to my mother's house, beyond Jonesboro,' she tells him, her voice strangely distant and very low. 'I'm late and fear I have lost my way.' 'I'll walk with you,' he offers, thinking that perhaps something interesting might come of his gallantry. She falls in step with him. After a few paces he notices the basket and, thinking it appears heavy, offers to carry it for her. 'You are a gentleman,' she says softly in that strangely distant voice. He slips his arm through the bale and there's weight to it, but a towel over it prevents him from viewing the contents.

"Well, then the woman begins to tease him, laughing at him, and to Donald MacFadden's shock, he realizes the laughter is coming from inside the basket. Lifting the towel, there inside the basket is the woman's taunting head. Shocked, he drops the basket, and the head rolls out and tumbles down to the misty water's edge.

"All at once the woman flings off her bonnet and there's nothing under it but her shoulders, while upon the ground lies that grinning head, laughing at him still! Shaken to the soles of his new boots, MacFadden takes off in a dead run, crying out in fright. Right behind him he hears her footsteps. Glancing over his shoulder, he sees the woman in hot pursuit, swinging the head by its long hair as she comes on. He runs wildly through the swirling fog, his heart pounding in his ears. Again he looks over his shoulder. She's closer this time, and just then she throws the head at him. It bounces on the road ahead of him and rolls about his feet, snarling and snapping at him, its teeth long like wolf fangs.

"They bite through his trousers, nipping at the tops

of his new boots, leaping at his legs, growling like a mad dog, tearing ragged holes in his clothing. It's only the boots that keep the teeth from sinking deep into his flesh. He can't shake that devil-possessed head as onward he runs, trying to kick it aside, and that woman is still right behind him!

"And now the head begins to howl like the hounds of the dead, and the sound of it rises up from the hollow and rings in the night air. Later, three different families claimed they heard it, and my father was one of them. To this very day he swears it was the sound of a lost soul out to find a mate, he does."

"What happened after that?" Conner asked.

Bodine's view grew distant. "MacFadden couldn't outrun the head, or the woman, and he knew he had to do something quickly. In desperation, he plunged into the swamp and wadded through those dark, sucking waters just as fast as his tired legs would carry him. The woman stopped at the water's edge, giving out a bone-chilling wail. When he looked back, she was just standing there, her head snapping about on the ground in pure frustration. She stood there watching him flee until the bog trees closed in behind him.

"MacFadden never stopped running until he made it all the way home that night. But the fright of the encounter was too much for him, and he collapsed on the porch in front of his very own door. His dear wife took him inside and laid him upon their bed. Terrified, he only just managed to tell her the terrible truth of what had happened, and then his terrified heart burst, and Donald MacFadden died."

Chapter Three

Bodine fell silent. There was not a sound inside the dugout cabin, just the crackle of their fire and the wind outside making a mournful wail. After a moment he went on softly, "Hillary says the headless woman got him after all. After they buried MacFadden, there began to be sightings of *two* people roaming the swamps after midnight: a tall woman with a basket over her arm, and a man wearing trousers, ragged about the legs where his black, shiny boots can be seen. Not even dogs will go there after sunset."

A shiver coursed through Kit. "What of Hillary?"

"She moved away from the Hollow shortly afterward and let the forest take back the farm. Moved into town, she did, and married the mayor a few months later, or so I heard. They both had left the county by the time I was old enough to be on my own."

"Saints," O'Farrell breathed.

Just then a sound carried upon the wind made them jump. It was a woman's wail . . . or at least so it sounded to the spooked men.

"What's that?" O'Farrell yelped.

Kit and Gray Feather exchanged glances and shook their heads. Conner reached for a pistol as their eyes shifted toward the blanket that covered the window. "Probably just the wind," Kit said finally. He gave a short laugh. "Bodine's tale's got us jumpier than a long-legged jackass rabbit at a coyote rendezvous."

They chuckled nervously. Conner set the pistol aside.

Gray Feather kept listening. "Didn't sound like the wind to me."

"Cut that out, Mr. Feather."

The cry reached them again, more distant this time. No one moved. Conner licked dry lips and said, "What . . . what sort of critter makes a sound like that, Kit?"

"Maybe it's a cat." He glanced again at the Ute.

"Maybe," Gray Feather allowed, "but if it is, it sure did have a human sound to it, unlike any cat I've ever heard."

Kit said, "I'm going to take a quick look around." He glanced at the ceiling. "Need to clear the snow off anyway, before we have it all in our laps."

Kit Carson shrugged into his heavy coat and grabbed up a pistol. Icy wind stabbed him to the bones as he trudged through the drifts that had piled up against the cabin. Squinting into the driving snow, he could only see a few feet in either direction. The snow was unbroken around the cabin, and if it had been some animal that had made the noise, it had left no sign.

He grinned to himself. Bodine's ghost story had gotten to him. "Jumpier than a jackass rabbit," he said to himself, and turned his attention to the roof, sweeping the snow from it with a bough. Gray Feather emerged from the cabin a few minutes later to give him a hand.

As the two men worked, Gray Feather said beneath his breath, "What are we going to do about Bodine?"

"It looks bad for him," he answered softly so the words wouldn't carry. "I've never seen a foot, a finger, or a hand that bad frostbit ever get better on its own."

"Nor have I."

Kit nodded for Gray Feather to follow him. They kicked a path through the drifts away from the cabin and stopped just before the trees closed in on the little clearing. Out of earshot the two men could discuss the matter without Bodine overhearing.

"You ever deal with bad frostbite, Gray Feather?"

"No, but I've seen men die from it in my village."

"There's not much that can be done for it once it begins to mortify. Not a pleasant way to go." Kit grimaced and looked into his friend's dark eyes. "There's only one thing to be done for a man when that happens."

"Maybe we can get him back to winter quarters first."

"Not likely. This storm's liable to keep us holed up here for a week or more."

Gray Feather thought a moment. "You ever do it before?"

Kit shook his head. "No. But I seen it done once— back in '26, on my first trip out to the mountains. We'd been on the Santa Fe trail but a few weeks when

39

a fellow named Broadus had an accident with his rifle. Shot himself in the arm while drawing it from the wagon to kill a wolf. Whal, the arm began to mortify, and Broadus was in such bad torment that he welcomed any remedy. We seen that it would be necessary to amputate the arm. I watched one of the men do it with a razor and an old saw. It wasn't a pleasant job, but one that had to be done. After the arm was cut off, we heated a king bolt of one of the wagons and burned the afflicted parts to stop the bleeding. Finished the stump off with a plaster of tar taken from off the wheel of a wagon."

"How did he fare?"

"Broadus recovered just fine. He was healthy and full of vinegar by the time we arrived in Santa Fe that November, getting along with one arm as if he was born that way."

"Could you amputate the leg, Kit?"

"It's not something I'd want to do, but given the choice of cutting off that leg or watching Bodine die, whal, I reckon I would—so long as he wanted it so."

"Maybe it won't come to that," Gray Feather said with subdued optimism.

Kit shook his head. "I'd be pleased if it didn't, but this child has seen it happen too many times to hold out much hope."

"How long you figure he has?"

Kit shook his head. "Don't know. But I do know we don't want the mortification to poison the blood. When that happens thar's nothing can be done. The pain will get so bad that Bodine will beg us to put him out of the misery."

"Tomorrow?"

Kit nodded gravely. "We'll likely need to come to some decision by then."

The raging storm still held the mountain in its icy death grip the next morning. After a cold night, a coating of ice crackled on the buffalo skins that covered the sleeping men. O'Farrell reached over and stirred the coals of their fire, feeding some kindling and blowing life into the fire again. In a few minutes heat began to fill the cabin, and one by one the men threw off their stiff blankets. The cabin filled with the steam of their breath until the heat finally pushed the cold back outside where it belonged.

Bodine had had a fitful night and was still sleeping. They tried not to wake him just yet as they put on coffee and boiled water.

Kit drew on his coat, gloves, and hat, not sure if they weren't colder than the air that awaited him outside. But in a few moments he warmed inside them and pushed his way out the door, clawing up through the bank of snow that had heaped outside it.

The morning sun was hidden somewhere beyond the storm clouds and the day was gray and depressing. A fierce wind still whipped snow across the clearing, but some of the strength had gone out of it. The cabin was nearly covered, and it took a supreme effort to climb through the deep drifts. His first task was to clear the roof again. After he finished that he checked on the horses.

The animals were huddled against the protection of a rocky outcropping, sharing their heat. The corral, too, was nearly covered. Kit walked over the top rail on a drift. Near where the horses stood the snow had piled nearly to the level of their knees, but in the lee of the tall rocks they had moved about enough to keep a spot open to stand in.

Kit fitted halters and took them down to a frozen creek that ran below the cabin. He kicked around until he had uncovered a boulder of about a hundred pounds, and, lifting it high above his head, he bashed a hole in the ice. While the horses drank, Kit thought of the injured man. Bodine would have to be given his choice today. How would he take it? Kit had known the man only a few months, and in that time he'd discovered that Andy Bodine was an easygoing fellow with a keen mind and quick wit. He had seen him get angry only once, and that was when O'Farrell had taken the doll and taunted him with it. What was it about the doll that had set the man off like it had? he wondered.

When the horses had taken their fill, Kit took a long drink of the icy water flowing beneath the crushed ice, then returned the horses to their corral. Afterward, he returned to the creek where cottonwood trees stood along its bank and with his tomahawk stripped off an armful of bark for the horses to eat.

Kit beat the snow from his clothes as best he could before crawling through the small door down into the dugout. The warm air inside was a pleasant greeting. Bodine was awake and sitting up, looking pained and worried. Kit arranged the door blanket and weighted it down with a piece of wood to keep the wind at bay.

"Coffee?" Conner offered.

Kit rubbed his chilled hands together and blew into

them. "Best offer I've had all day." The hot cup felt good, and he held it in both hands, absorbing as much heat from it as he could. "Did I ever mention I'm getting too old for this kind of winter?"

"Only about once every other day," Gray Feather noted.

Kit laughed and sipped the coffee. It tasted good and warmed him all the way down. "We need to put in more firewood. I busted a hole in the ice below for the horses. It's still open, if anyone's interested.

"We're getting by with melted snow just fine, Mr. Carson," O'Farrell said. "And I don't fancy anyone here is inclined to use that hole to take a bath now."

They laughed. Kit grinned and slanted an eye toward Bodine. "How you feeling this morning, Andy?"

"I'm . . . I'm doing all right, Kit."

The mountain man scowled at him. "Aren't much of a liar, are you?"

Bodine frowned at the coffee cup in his hand, then handed it to Conner. "Mind?"

Conner filled it from the pot on the coals and put it carefully in Bodine's fingers. It trembled slightly as he lifted to his lips. After he'd taken a sip he said, "Fact of the matter is, I'm not feeling all that good, Kit."

"Leg hurts?"

"No. Surprisingly, I don't feel it at all." His voice was low, even, and without the playful bantering that had been there the day before.

"Feeling sick about the belly, are you? And your head is beginning to feel like a smithy's shaping a horseshoe on it?"

"Yeah. That pretty much describes it. You know what it means?"

Kit glanced at the grim faces watching him and Bodine. "I think so. Think everyone here knows what it means. Even Conner, and he's about as green to the mountains as a fresh willow twig in spring."

Bodine stiffened.

"And you know it too," Kit went on soberly.

"I don't want to hear it."

"All right, I won't say the words. But you best be thinking about them. Time is coming real soon when we're going to have to have us a serious powwow on the matter, Andy."

Bodine looked away, and the crackling fire and wind outside sounded louder than they were.

"I think I'll go find us some wood," Conner offered, grabbing for his coat.

"I'll go with you," Gray Feather said, and the two men ducked under the low door and disappeared.

Bodine stared at the cup in his hands.

Kit caught the frown deepening into Sean O'Farrell's face an instant before the man turned his head away from him. O'Farrell was regretting what had befallen Bodine—regretting it mostly because he realized full well he had been the cause of it. But the man's pride kept him from admitting so now.

Toward noon the storm abated some and the howling wind eased. Peeling back the blanket that covered the window, Kit batted away the snow that had piled up against the side of the cabin. He could see nearly across the valley that lay before them. To his right the horses were huddled against the rocks that had given them some protection from the biting wind. To his left the tall pines were white and bent with the heavy snow that drooped their boughs low to the ground. In places the snow had piled three feet or more, with drifts climbing higher than that. And although the wind had died down, snow was still falling heavily.

O'Farrell said, "A wee bit of a break in this storm. I think I'll take advantage of it and try to shoot us some fresh meat." He bundled up and took his shooting bag and rifle from the corner where they had been stacked.

"Don't wander too far," Kit advised. "If the wind picks up again, you won't know which way is back."

"I'll not be straying too far, Mr. Carson," he said, and left.

Kit arranged the blanket after him, weighing it down to keep as much heat in the place as possible.

After O'Farrell had gone, Bodine said, "I'm making Sean nervous. I think he'd be more comfortable holed up with a grizzly bear than me right now."

"Can you blame him?" Conner replied. "He's feeling guilty. He knows it's his fault you're hurt, but his damned Irish arrogance won't let him own up to it."

"It's not all his fault," Bodine said. "No one made me ride off in a huff. I lost my temper." He paused. When he spoke next, his voice was low and thoughtful. "Something I haven't done in a lot of years." His eyes lifted and fixed upon his hunting bag, hanging on the wall with the others.

O'Farrell returned a few hours later with two rabbits, but nothing larger. Still, it was fresh meat for their cook pot, and welcomed. With the coming of night the wind picked up again, howling through the chinks in the logs and past the buffalo coats hung there to keep it out. But the snow, at least, had begun to taper off, and snatches of sky and moon could be seen through the ragged breaks in the scudding clouds.

The men sat around the fire listening to the moaning wind and rattling tree branches. The shadows from its flames played across their faces and danced upon the rough logs that protected them against the howling weather beyond.

Bodine was in growing distress. A squeezing ache that he could only describe as "a fist tightening about his calf" had begun to creep up his leg, and he was trying hard to endure it in silence. He had started to run a low fever, too, and Kit knew it would only get worse, not better.

As if sensing a need for some diversion from the gloomy mood that had overtaken them, Gray Feather said suddenly, "I've been thinking about that story Andy told yesterday."

"Don't tell me you've met a headless woman too?" Conner chided.

When they stopped laughing, Gray Feather merely shook his head. Unruffled, he said, "No woman, but there are stories among my people of some pretty strange creatures hiding up in these mountains."

"You mean that . . . that sound we heard last night?" O'Farrell asked.

"It was no animal I've ever encountered," he said.

"What sort of strange critters?" Kit asked.

"I'm thinking about one in particular. It was told of a creature that lives in the north country. It's called a Wendigo."

"A *Wendigo*, Mr. Feather? What sort of creature might that be?"

Gray Feather shook his head. "Whatever it is, it's not what we think of as being real."

"Aye, of another world? Of an earlier world? Like the wee folk of the fairy mound?"

"Maybe."

"What do you know of the critter?" Kit asked.

"The story I heard was about three hunters who were going out after moose. Two were Englishmen of the old Northwest Company. The third was their Indian pathfinder named Defago. They had traveled a couple days and were camped one night on the banks of some nameless, frozen lake. Well, during the day the Indian got to feeling uneasy, claimed to smell strange odors, things he couldn't identify—"

"Otherworldly smells," O'Farrell interjected.

"Perhaps. Whatever they were, it made the guide nervous, and he kept peering off into the forest, thinking he heard sounds right behind him. Whenever he looked, there was nothing. They crawled into their tipi for the night, and no sooner had they closed it up tight than a mighty wind began to blow. It was colder than death, and it shook the tipi mightily. They could hear the trees rustling against one another, creaking in the blasts. One of the hunters was curious, and wanting to see the storm better, and he opened the flap."

"What did he see, Mr. Feather?"

"Nothing. The air was perfectly still. The trees without a breath of wind touching their branches. And the quiet was unnatural, as if no animal dare be caught there, as if sound itself had ceased to exist."

"Saints!"

"But then it gets really strange, for inside the tipi the storm still raged, the skins shook, the lodgepoles rattled. And carried upon the wind, a soft sighing that was really a word, a single word being spoken over and over again: 'Defago . . . Defago . . . De-faa-goooo . . . '

"Defago cowered under his blankets until he could take no more. Suddenly he cried that his feet were on fire! They were fiery wings, and he must fly away! Before the Englishmen could stop him, Defago dove out the door and disappeared into the forest. The next day they searched for him, following his tracks. They discovered a curious thing, for once beyond the campsite, Defago's tracks were followed by another set, a huge set! And as they followed them further, the huge tracks became more human, while Defago's became more . . . more creaturelike, I'd reckon you could say."

Gray Feather paused, only to discover every eye upon him. He grinned and said, "The hunters never did find Defago, and finally they made their way back to the fort. When they told the story, the Indians there said it sounded to them like the Wendigo got him. They said the Wendigo comes with the wind, and if he gets hold of you, he drags you so fast that your feet burn away. Then all the rest of you, too."

"That's a tall tale if I've ever heard one," Conner said.

"Is it?"

Kit saw that Gray Feather was not completely convinced it wasn't a yarn.

"The story goes on."

"Finish it," O'Farrell said. His voice was a whisper, and there was the fire of wonder in his eyes.

"Defago showed up at the fort some weeks later, his feet badly burned, babbling like a fool. No one could make any sense of what he was saying. But they did understand one word. It was *Wendigo*. He just kept repeating it, and a few days later he died."

Conner just shook his head. Kit had a hard time believing it too, but O'Farrell had taken the tale as truth, and was shaken by it.

"There are other tales," Gray Feather went on. "They are too widespread to be mere legends. Every tribe has its own 'Wendigo,' or something similar. They go by different names, but they all describe the same creature. Sioux have their *Chiye tanka*. The Shoshones call him *T'so' apittse*. Yakamas know him as *Ste ye hah*. The Chinooks, *Skookum*. He has been called the 'evil god of the woods,' or 'wild man,' or 'big hairy man.' Some just call him the 'mountain demon.' But whatever name he's known as, the descriptions are always the same: a huge, hairy, manlike creature. Some say he's a cannibal. Others claim he torments women. Details are different, but there are just too many stories for them all to be legends and fables."

"Mountain demon," O'Farrell repeated, glancing toward the blanketed window. "Saints," he breathed.

When the men crawled into their blankets later, it was with an ear tuned to the wind outside, and perhaps a silent prayer that none would hear his name being whispered upon it.

A sound snapped Kit from a fitful sleep, and he lay beneath the heavy coat and blanket a long while, staring into the darkness. The fire had burned down to a bed of coals, which filled the little cabin with an eerie red glow.

There it was again. A crunch upon the snow outside, a tap against the wall of the cabin. Ears straining, Kit tried to identify the noise that had intruded upon his sleep. All around him came the soft breathing of the sleeping men. From Bodine came the occasional groan from the pain of the dying limb. But that hadn't been what had awakened him. There was something outside.

Down in the corral their horses had begun to whinny nervously.

Quietly Kit crawled out of his blanket and slipped into his coat. Moving carefully so as not to wake the others, he felt for and found his Hawken pistol and slipped out the door.

He crouched near the opening, his view sweeping the unbroken white landscape before him. The snow had stopped falling, but the wind's cold touch swirled around him, ruffling the shaggy fur coat, tugging at his badger-skin hat, which hung down to his shoulders. Overhead the clouds had broken apart and moved across the sky like long, gnarled fingers. The moon's pale light reached down past them, giving a soft glow to the valley below.

In the corral their horses were moving nervously about. They sensed him and turned, watching him with ears laid back and steam surging from their nostrils.

Kit stepped cautiously away from the cabin, feeling a spider crawl up his spine. Perhaps it had been the sound of a coyote scrounging for food that had awakened him, or maybe a cougar. Or perhaps it was nothing at all. A tight grin creased Kit's face. A bit of Bodine's groaning, a smattering of Gray Feather's Wendigo story . . .

Kit listened, but did not hear his name being called on the wind.

There were no new tracks in the snow that he could see. Only those made earlier while the men were gathering wood and tending to their animals.

The horses milled about the tiny piece of open ground.

Kit's fist tightened around the pistol as his eyes shifted across the barren, snow-covered ground. He stepped into the tracks and started toward the corral. The path took him past a stand of aspen trees, their naked branches rattling in the wind like a bag of dead man's bones, the shadows piled up beneath them untouched by the broken moonlight.

A horse whinnied again. Something was making the animals nervous.

Then a movement to Kit's right made him spin around. His eyes probed the shadows and saw nothing. Was his brain playing tricks on him? A flicker of movement caught his eye deep in the forest. Kit went rigid, and his heart leaped to this throat. Skimming across the snow was something—something like the shape of a woman, or so he thought at first. Her long hair was fluttering in the wind behind her, and her clothes seemed to drift up as if buoyed by some unseen hand.

But it could not be a woman, or a man, for it moved too swiftly across the deep snow. Kit blinked to make sure. The shock of seeing the apparition held him there. It wasn't a woman, couldn't be a woman! Even though the distance was great, nearly at the edge of his vision, he was certain that although the creature, whatever it was, was running on two legs like a human, it had upon its head a rack of antlers like that of a deer or elk!

Chapter Four

In the light of a new day the land gleamed crisp, white, and clean. The wind had stopped blowing sometime during the night, and it looked to Kit Carson as if this might be another reprieve from the storm that had mounted an almost unceasing attack on these mountains for more than a week. A permanent reprieve, he hoped.

He brought the animals to water and fed them more of the tough cottonwood bark, which was neither very nourishing nor very good for them, but common enough fare for grazing animals in the dead of winter when any grass was buried beneath a yard of snow.

Afterward, he broke a path through the snow to the stand of aspens and stood there staring into them. Their leafless branches stood in stark contrast against the clear blue sky. In the daylight they did not remind him of a bag of bones at all. He peered toward where he had seen the strange apparition the night before.

On this bright morning the memory of it seemed only a bad dream to him. He laughed out loud and watched the steam of his breath dissipate before his eyes. He was certain he had seen something, but the night plays tricks on a man's eyes. Whatever it was, he was sure in the light of day he could find some reasonable explanation.

His curiosity aroused, he trudged through the deep snow toward the place where he had seen it. The night wind would have covered most tracks, but he was determined to make a search just the same. At one point he found what may have been the footprints of the apparition, but they had been covered with blown snow, just as he feared, and were hard to make out. They appeared too large to be human. From what he could decipher from the faint impressions, there were three toes in front and one behind. They were unlike anything he had ever seen before, and he'd have reckoned a giant chicken had made them if he didn't know that was impossible. They led off in the right direction, however, and he would have followed them if the others were not waiting for him back at the cabin.

That thought was a sudden burden to his spirit.

Bodine had awoken in a bad way that morning. The pain had grown intolerable, and a fever had him in sweats. They had waited long enough. The mortified leg would have to come off, and it would have to be done today. Leaving the mystery of his night vision unsolved, Kit retraced his steps, gathering firewood where he could find it as he made his way back to the cabin.

Conner was cooling Bodine's forehead with a damp rag when he returned. "How you feeling?" Kit asked, taking off a glove and pressing a hand to the man's forehead. "You're all afire, my friend."

"I got the misery in real bad way, Kit," Bodine croaked, dragging a tongue over his pale lips.

Kit shed his coat and hunkered down by the injured man. Conner, Gray Feather, and O'Farrell knew what must come next, but they seemed to be waiting for Kit to do the talking. He grimaced and said, "Remember what I told you yesterday?"

Bodine grimaced, fear tightening the skin around his eyes and mouth.

"You remember. I said I wouldn't mention it then, but the time has come. Told you to be thinking about it. Whal, time's come to grab the bull by the horns."

Bodine swallowed down a hard lump. "Could it wait till we get back to winter quarters?"

"Thar's three to four feet of snow out thar. It would take our horses days to break a trail through it back to winter quarters. And that's if the storm doesn't roll back in. And you ain't got days. That leg has mortified and is filling you up with poison, Andy. If it don't come off, and soon, it'll take you down just as sure as a bullet from my buffler rifle."

Bodine must have seen something humorous in that, for in spite of his failing condition he managed a faint smile. "I might wish for the bullet instead. Least I'd go down quick."

Conner said, "It'll be all right, Andy. Once it's over,

the pain will go away. Shoot, lots of men get along on one leg."

"Aye! And all men will call you Peg Leg. Peg Leg Bodine will be your name, and that will be some honor indeed," O'Farrell added, trying to encourage him.

"An honor I'd gladly give to any one of you gents," Bodine answered. He held Kit in his piercing stare. "Who here can do it?"

The men looked at Kit. The mountain man gave a wry smile and said, "Appears like I've been volunteered."

"You ever do it before?"

"Why, sure I have. Ever hear of a fellow by the name of Andrew Broadus?"

"No."

"Whal, I took his arm off—whal, with the help of some others." That wasn't exactly true, but this wasn't the time or place to parse words, and it seemed to make Bodine feel better.

"You did? How did it go?"

"Easy as falling off a log, Andy. Broadus hardly felt it at all. And after a couple days he was making do like he never knew he ever had another arm in the first place. He did just fine, and so will you."

Bodine stared at the ceiling, his throat bobbing a couple times. "It'll hurt powerful bad. Ain't even got a pint of whiskey to ease the pain."

"I ain't going to tell you it won't, Andy. But the pain will pass. You're hurting bad now, and that won't pass unless you take the remedy. That leg is gonna kill you. This ol' coon has seen it happen to other men."

Bodine gave a short laugh. "Always figured when I

went under it would be to a Injun's arrow. Never figured it would be my own body what turned against me."

"You know what we do with turncoats, Andy," Gray Feather said.

"That's right," Conner added. "We give them the rope."

"Or the knife?" Bodine quipped.

"Whatever it takes," Conner went on. "I'll be right here with Kit. I won't let nothing go wrong, Andy."

"You're a good friend, Tom. I know you'll do what you can." A stab of pain cut his words short, and his teeth clenched behind his drawn lips.

Kit said to O'Farrell, "Build that fire up and get some more water to boiling." To Gray Feather he said, "Look through our saddlebags and see what you can find for bandages."

"Tom, hand me that tomahawk."

"Tomahawk?" He glanced suspiciously at Bodine's leg, then at the short ax wedged in a length of firewood. Wordlessly, the young trapper jerked it free and passed it across. Kit went to work on it with his knife, prying the locking wedge from the top of the hickory haft and hammering the iron head off of it. When he finished, he did the same to his own ax.

Gray Feather had recovered a cotton shirt from O'Farrell's bag. The Irishman watched as Kit cut it into strips, never lifting his voice once to object.

"I want a bed of right hot coals, Sean," Kit said.

"They'll be so hot, the devil hisself will cry out for mercy."

They set out a pair of whetstones, and Kit and Gray Feather got busy drawing a keen edge on the blades of their butcher knives. No one spoke more than was necessary. The gravity of the chore ahead was a heavy stone upon each of them. Bodine had closed his eyes against their preparations and seemed to be trying to prepare himself for the ordeal to come. His lips moved, but whatever speaking he was doing, it was inside his head. Even so, it was plain that he was sending up a passel of prayers, and Kit added one of his own to the stream.

"I've got it ten times hotter than hell," O'Farrell told him. Kit placed the two Tomahawk heads in the heart of the coals and the two hafts within easy reach.

Knives sharpened, bandages prepared, hot water and cloths close at hand, Kit said, "Andy?"

Bodine opened an eye, and the moisture there was more than the sweat of the fever. "Lord, Kit. Do it quick. Do it clean. And don't let me make a blubbering fool of myself."

"You bellow and squall as much as you need to, Andy. I'll do all I can for you."

Bodine's sweat-glistened head nodded. Kit inclined his head, and Conner and O'Farrell each grabbed an arm. Gray Feather sat upon Bodine's good leg while taking a firm grip upon the gangrenous one.

"Lord, Lord, Lord," Bodine murmured until Kit pushed a stick between his teeth.

"Bite down hard."

His teeth sunk into the tough wood. Kit positioned one of the knives above the joint of the knee. He took a breath to calm himself. The salty taste of sweat was in the corners of his mouth. He knew what he had to do, and that it had to be done quickly. He hoped Bodine would pass out from the pain—but there was no guarantee. Andrew Broadus's cries of torment of all those years ago flooded back into his brain. Kit took another breath, then a third, and put the blade to Bodine's knee. . . .

The scream rang out through the forest, echoing against its deep, frozen silence. It was a fearful, horrifying sound that lasted a full five minutes before suddenly going quiet.

Among a bramble beneath the snow-laden trees, a head jerked up and peered intently in the cabin's direction. The creature's dark eyes never blinked, never wavered from that small thread of smoke where the *new ones* were denned up. It squatted motionless in the deep snow, listening, wondering . . . curious.

Then the wailing stopped.

Only then did the creature blink. It thought a moment, head canted to one side. Deciding, it abandoned the serviceberry bush where it had been clawing up the snow in search of last year's dried berries and cautiously, soundlessly, stole across the snow toward the now silent cabin.

Once Bodine passed out, the unpleasant job became easier. Without having to fight against the leg twisting and wrenching in pain, Kit's knife was able to work its way quickly through the joint in Bodine's knee. They had no saw to cut bone, so the knee was the only way to get the job done in a hurry and cleanly.

The cabin became deadly silent. No man spoke, every eye riveted on the gruesome task at hand. When

Kit called for a warm, wet rag to clean up the blood, it was passed to him wordlessly.

Thomas Conner wore a vaguely ill expression as he held the arm of his friend, which no longer thrashed about. O'Farrell seemed in a trance. Gray Feather appeared unmoved by the operation, his attention focused, his mouth set in a tight, determined line across his face. He was nearest the fire and immediately ready to hand Kit whatever it was he asked for.

Kit tried to detach himself from the task as best he could, picturing in his mind a buffalo or elk beneath his knife as it sawed through tendons, muscles, and arteries that gushed a fountain of blood across the cabin before Gray Feather could pinch them shut.

After he had parted leg from man, Kit set the mortified limb aside and brought a handle to one of the tomahawk heads glowing dull red in the coals. When he slipped the haft into the eye the wood burst instantly into flames. Driving the handle against a rock to set the head, Kit pressed the flat of the blade to raw flesh. Smoke, and the stench of burning flesh, filled the cabin. Even Gray Feather had to look away—but only for an instant. Kit repeated the procedure with the second ax head, careful to cauterize the big artery and vein, and all the smaller vessels that seeped blood. When he was satisfied with the job, he cleaned the stump and wrapped it in a scrap of cotton cloth that had been a shirt only a little while before.

He had lost track of time. The ordeal was over, and Kit had no notion as to whether an hour had passed, or only fifteen minutes.

O'Farrell let go of a long breath, as if he had been holding it all the while. "You did a fine job of it, Mr. Carson. You missed your calling. Maybe you should have been a surgeon instead of a trapper?"

"No, thank you, sir. This child hopes he never sees the day when he has to do this again."

"I'm . . . I'm not feeling too good," Conner said, going pale in the face. "Is Andy going to be all right?"

"It's wait and see now."

"He fainted away like he up and died."

"It was the best thing that could have happened to him," Gray Feather allowed.

Conner swallowed hard a couple time, his breathing quickening.

"Go outside and breathe some fresh air," Kit said.

"Yes. I think so." He didn't waste a moment. He grabbed his coat and carried it out the low door with him.

"A weak stomach that lad has," O'Farrell said with a laugh.

"He's just sensitive," Gray Feather noted. "And sensitivity is a trait we could use more of around here."

O'Farrell frowned. "All right. You made your point, Mr. Feather. Now, what do we do next?"

Kit looked at his bloody hands. "Now I wash up in some of that hot water." He mixed in a little snow to cool it and scrubbed the blood from his fingers, from under his nails, and wiped what he could off his clothes.

A soft groan escaped Bodine's lips as his head

rolled from side to side. They watched him, expecting consciousness to return any moment, but then the low, mournful sound stopped and his eyes stayed closed.

"It's best if he sleeps a while longer," O'Farrell said softly.

Kit finished cleaning up, then stopped all at once to listen.

"What is it?" Gray Feather asked.

"Either of you two coons hear a peep out of Conner yet?"

Neither had.

Kit frowned.

"Aw, what kind of trouble can he get into?" O'Farrell said.

The Irishman was right. What could go wrong out there, after all? Kit shrugged off the warning that had crept into his brain and finished cleaning up. Then he looked at Bodine's leg, still off to the side where he had set it.

"What are you going to do with that?" O'Farrell asked.

Gray Feather gave a short laugh. "Maybe Andy will want to keep it as a souvenir?"

"Aye! Mr. Feather, you have a sick sense of humor."

Kit said, "I can use some fresh air myself. I'll take it outside and far away from the cabin. I've been thinking we might have coyotes or cougars prowling the neighborhood, or a pack of scavenging wolves. I don't want it lying around to attract them. You two see to him if he wakes up."

"We will," Gray Feather answered for both of them.

"He'll be in a powerful lot of pain and might be a handful."

"We can handle Mr. Bodine. You just be taking that thing far away from here, Mr. Carson. I don't want it to be attracting any beasties our way, whether they be of the living or the other kind, if you be knowing what I mean."

"You mean the ghost of the missing leg?" Kit grinned.

"All right, you can be making fun of it now, Mr. Carson, but someday you will see, and then believe. These very eyes of mine have beheld such thing back in Erin as you can hardly imagine."

Still grinning, Kit ducked under the door, fixed the blanket back in place, and stood. The glaring snow made him momentarily blind. When he could see again there was only snow and more snow in every direction. Footprints led down to the horse corral, where the animals mulled about, digging with their hooves to uncover buried grasses and shrubs. Another set of tracks led off in the opposite direction, the trail Conner had just made. Kit studied the situation some. The ground was frozen solid and impossible to dig. Burying the leg was out of the question. The only other choice was to carry it into the forest and stash it up in a tree, out of reach of most four-footed predators.

Kit squinted down the fresh trail and called to Conner, but the man did not answer. Kit was distantly aware of that vague, uncomfortable feeling working its way to the front of his brain again. Not quite a warning—at least not yet—but somehow disturbing nonetheless.

He called for Conner a second time. When he got no reply, he shrugged, hitched the leg under his arm, and started into the forest, trudging through the deep snow into the dark forest that frowned down at the little, half-buried cabin.

Chapter Five

Kit didn't intend to go far, but he knew that the scent of decaying flesh would draw animals from miles around, especially after this snowstorm had buried any easy food. Right now this was a mountain full of hungry critters, he mused. A few hundred yards ought be far enough from the cabin to keep them from making a pest of themselves. Kit thought of Bodine, lying back there with half a leg missing. If the man did pull through the ordeal, they would have to remain here at least another week before they could carry him out on a travois.

He glanced at the patches of sky visible beyond the towering, glistening, snow-laden pine boughs. Not a cloud in sight. Maybe this really was the end to the storm. He hoped so. Another big one rolling down from the north might keep them penned up here a month or more.

As Kit broke a path through the snow, the absolute silence of the place struck him again, just as it had the first day, before they had found Bodine and made their way to the cabin. It was unnaturally quiet. Big snowstorms were often like that afterward. There was the crunch of snow beneath his feet and the frequent swishing of cascading slides from overladen boughs, and that was all. Not even a whisper of wind.

An uneasiness, like someone was following him, or eyes were watching him, made its way to the fore of his thoughts. With each step he took, the more oppressive and troubling the feeling became. When he stopped to look, nothing was there. He wished suddenly he had brought a gun along, but at the time it had seemed unnecessary. He was going only a short distance. Still, it had been foolish of him to leave it behind, even if they had not seen hide nor hair of a single hostile Indian in months. The uneasiness was nothing more than a stoked-up imagination shrugging off the remnants of a few good ghost stories and a rather grisly task, he told himself. Just the same, Kit began to look for a convenient place to stash the limb and be done with it. A few yards more.

He was breathing heavy from the trek through the deep snow. All at once he stopped and stared beyond the steam of his own breath.

Built of poles and covered with snow, it blended so well with the background that Kit had almost looked right past it. Again that spider crawled up his spine and he shivered. Was it only the cold? Casting quickly about, all he saw was endless forest cloaked in its sparkling mantle of white. That didn't explain the notion, now stronger than before, that he was not alone.

It was a scaffold in a clearing among a stand of aspen trees. Kit had seen similar structures a time or two before. It was a burial pallet. As he drew closer he could see that a body still remained atop this one. Oftentimes bodies were placed on such scaffolds and allowed to decay. Then their bones would be taken to a secret place and buried. The wrapped body upon this burial scaffold had not yet decayed. He had probably died that fall and the cold had preserved him.

Kit forced his way through deep drifts that put him on a level with the blanket-wrapped form visible beneath the snow that covered it. Wind had kept the pallet fairly clear. The blanket was frozen stiff and unable to be moved, but by the size of it, Kit judged it to be the body of a man. The crude pallet and simple wrapping told him it had not been a man of great importance; no chief lay here, nor any notable warrior.

On a whimsy, Kit placed Andy Bodine's leg on the pallet alongside the corpse. "Here you are, buck," he said, grinning. "Some company so you aren't all alone a-way out here. Your people all go off and leave you?"

He got no reply, and was deeply grateful for that. He suspected the body might be that of a Blackfoot. Maybe one of the many who had fallen to the small-pox plague. Smallpox had devastated the tribes this year, driving them far north, leaving the trappers to work in peace for the first time in as many years as Kit could recall.

Kit left the pallet, retracing his steps back to the cabin. He had gone no more than fifty feet when something in the snow caught his eye. Leaving the trail, Kit crossed unbroken snow to the place where a set of tracks had crushed the snow. They were huge, a good two feet long. Oddly formed, somehow unnatural looking. They were not well defined, for snow had filled in a good portion of them, but Kit had seen these tracks before. There were three toes forward and one back, but there also appeared to be a webbing of some sort between the toes. Instead of a huge chicken, Kit thought of a huge duck.

Neither made any sense. If only he could find one fresh and clear set of tracks to study. He was certain he would know what had made them. But whatever it was, he was convinced of one thing. For all its apparent size, it could not have weighed very much. The tracks weren't deep enough. Kit recalled the apparition he had seen the night before. It had been man-shaped, except for the antlers. He remembered how it seemed to almost float across the snow, as a man wearing snowshoes might. . . .

Suddenly that feeling was back. It was strong this time. Much stronger. The hairs at the nape of his neck began to bristle, as they always did when danger lurked nearby. His hand moved slowly for the knife at his side.

It wasn't there! He had left that behind with his guns and his tomahawk, and he was completely unarmed!

Ears straining, Kit caught the soft crunch of snow behind him. The faint sounds of breathing reached him, and then a shadow loomed across the snow.

Bunching fingers into a hard fist, Kit stood and whirled around.

"Whoa!" Thomas Conner cried, throwing up his arms to protect himself.

"It's you?" Kit was barely able to rein in the fist. He drew in a long, ragged breath. "Conner! What the devil are you doing sneaking up on a man like that? Don't you know if this child had had a gun you'd have likely had your brains blowed out by now?"

Conner stammered. "I—I didn't mean nothing by it, Kit. You called to me, didn't you? I heard you."

Kit was shaking from his racing heart and the rush of fight or flight surging through his system. "Don't you know you never come up on a man's backside without announcing that you're thar?"

"I guess I wasn't thinking."

"Wasn't thinking? That's the straight of it!" Kit drew in a long, calming breath. "Whal, no harm done this time. Only remember to call a warning before coming up on a man or a camp, or next time you're likely to go under with a bullet parting those gray eyes of yours."

"I'll remember. Reckon I'm still sorta green to mountain ways, Kit."

"Sorta? Huh! Whal, you'll learn . . . if you live long enough." Kit unknotted his fists. "If you heard me, why didn't you answer my call instead of sneaking like that?"

"I wasn't sneaking. I was just walking. And the reason I didn't answer you right away was, well . . . " Conner looked embarrassed. "Well, after watching what you did to Andy, my stomach wasn't just right anymore. I was busy getting sick."

Kit grimaced and was sorry he had snapped at the

young fellow. "That's nothing to be ashamed of, Tom. It wasn't easy for any of us to watch."

"Yes, I know. But it was *me* who retched up my guts because of it."

"Whal, forget it. I won't say a word to the others." Kit nodded his head toward the tracks. "Take a look here at what I found. You ever see anything like this?"

Conner hunkered over them and after a moment said, "No, never have. They don't look like no tracks any animal ever made. What are they?"

"Haven't figured that out yet, but you're right. Those are no animal tracks—least, no animal this child ever laid eyes on."

"They aren't human, either."

Kit's frown deepened.

"What could they be from? What sort of creature could have made them?"

"I don't know, and I'm not so all-fire sure I want to find out, either."

"Tell me again how big these tracks were that you say you found?" O'Farrell asked, a note of suspicion edging his voice.

Kit held his hand about two feet apart. "About this long."

"Nah! Nothing alive in these mountains could have left a print that long." O'Farrell narrowed an eye at him and said, "You be pulling my leg now, aren't you? Say it's so."

Gray Feather had ridden with Kit long enough to see that Kit wasn't greening them. "Three toes forward and one back?" the Ute asked, just to be certain he had heard the description right. "Webbed in between?"

"They weren't real clear. Edges broken and filled with snow. But that was the best I could judge it."

"He's right," Conner put in. "I saw them too."

O'Farrell scrunched his mouth tight around the stem of a clay pipe and pumped a volume of smoke into the air. He didn't take easily to being trifled with, and he wasn't about to buy Kit's tale hook, line, and sinker—not just yet, at least. "And you say there's a dead Injun out there too?"

"That's not so unusual these days. The pox has left a trail of them clear to the Canadian border," Gray Feather said.

O'Farrell's view shifted off Gray Feather and narrowed at Conner. The younger man merely shrugged his shoulders. "I didn't see the Indian, only the tracks."

O'Farrell considered a moment, then said, "Bah! You're both in on this tale."

Just then Bodine groaned, rolled his head, and opened one eye. The groan exploded to a shriek of pain, and immediately Kit and Conner leaped to hold him down.

"Take it easy, Andy," Kit said, his voice low and calming. "Thrashing around like this is only gonna hurt you some more."

"My leg!"

"It's gone. The poison won't hurt you anymore, but you got to rest easy. You don't want it to commence to bleeding again. That will just make it hurt worse."

Bodine clenched his teeth and, struggling against the torment, willed his head back down upon the saddle seat that served as his pillow. "The pain—can't hardly bear it, Kit."

"I know, but it'll get better. I promise you it will."

Bodine was panting, sweating. The fever had not broken yet, and that was worrisome. If it didn't eventually subside, it would be just as deadly as the mortified leg had been. "You just try to lie quiet. I know it hurts, Andy, but you got to try. Thirsty?"

The injured trapper squeezed his eyes shut, nodded, and licked his cracked lips. Kit tilted a cup of snowmelt to them and let Bodine take his fill of the cold water. "Thar you go. Drink it down slow. We're boiling jerky into a broth for you, and it'll be ready directly. I don't want you to take whole food yet, not until I see as you can keep it down."

"My leg . . . it feels all on fire."

"Had to cauterize the arteries, Andy. Had no choice in the matter."

Conner gripped the man's arm and said, "I'll be at your side, Andy. Anything you need, just tell me."

Bodine nodded and said, "Did . . . did it go good? Any troubles?"

"Kit did a dandy job of it, Andy. It bled some, but we got it stopped. Now you just need to rest and get better."

"I could surely use a drink," he croaked.

Conner reached for the water, but Bodine grabbed his arm. "No, I mean a *real* drink."

"Aye, couldn't we all," O'Farrell lamented.

The rest of the afternoon was spent seeing to Bodine's needs, keeping him warm, fed, and as comfortable as a man who had just lost a leg to a butcher knife could be kept.

They pulled back the blanket that covered the window opening. Although the air outside was frigid, it was dead still, and a warm sun burned in the clear sky, pouring its warmth through the little opening. Bodine said it felt good where it fell upon his blankets, so they left it open and kept the fire stoked up and the cabin filled with its heat. Throughout the afternoon they scrounged firewood, but no one ventured very far from the cabin, and none went without his rifle or a pistol tucked under his belt.

No one mentioned the tracks the rest of the afternoon, and Kit wondered if they really believed the story he and Conner had brought back. Even if they doubted it, no one was taking any chances. Gray Feather had examined each of the rifles in the corner, cleaning the flasholes and putting new caps on the nipples.

Later, as the sun was going down, O'Farrell finally brought up the subject. It was plain the tale had weighed heavy on his mind all day, and he was determined to clear the matter up once and for all.

"You know, Mr. Carson, I'd like to see these tracks, and that dead Indian, if you don't mind."

Kit had been helping Bodine with a cup of hot broth. "Getting too late now. Be dark in twenty minutes," he said. "But I'll take you to see them in the morning if you want."

"Tracks? Dead Indian?" This was the first Bodine had heard of them. The hours had taken the edge off his horrible pain, and he was more alert, and mastering his misery heroically. Kit briefly told him what he had discovered out behind the cabin.

"Do you believe there's some kind of monstrous critter prowling this mountainside? Something no one's ever seen before?" Bodine asked, his eyes suddenly wide and more wary than they had been all day.

"I didn't say that, Andy. To tell the truth, this child don't know what made those tracks, but I'm not jumping to any conclusions. I can't see how it can be a monster of any kind, seeing as the tracks it left didn't crush in the snow but a few inches."

"There's nothing alive that can leave a print that size," Conner declared. "It must be something else."

O'Farrell said, "I'm not so sure about that." They looked at him and he continued, his eyes staring, but not at them, not at anything in particular. "My grandfather told me of a time when he was but a lad. A monster had moved into the countryside, and it lived in the Coney Warren near a lake called Lough Graney. It was called a carrog, and it stood taller than the thatch on the roof of my grandfather's cottage. It had big, horrible teeth, a tail like a grand tree, and feet that had three toes sticking out in front. It would come and kill the sheep, swallowing them down whole, in one bite. Arrows and musket balls couldn't kill it, for they bounced right off its skin, which was all covered in scales, like armor plating, it was."

O'Farrell paused and looked at each of them. "Could that thing out there be a carrog?"

A long silence ticked off the seconds. Bodine said, "You don't believe that, do you?"

"Why not? Me grandfather saw it with his own two eyes. And I've seen dragons myself when I was a lad."

74

"Dragons?" Kit asked.

"Aye. Dragons. I was traveling with me uncle Daniel one summer when I was ten or eleven. We were in the neighborhood of Penllin Castle, at Glamorgan, when we come upon a rookery of dragons sleeping there in the sun upon the rocks."

"What did they look like?" Gray Feather asked.

"Like serpents, Mr. Feather. Just like great, coiled serpents, five feet long, roosting there in the warm sunlight. Their wings were folded back against their sides, and they were covered all over with sparkling scales. Red and gold and green, they were. And some, I think they might have been the males, had crests that shone like the rainbow. And when me uncle tossed a cobble into their midst, they jumped to the sky, flapping their leathery wings, sparkling all over with eyes like you see on a peacock's feather."

Kit was about to scoff at the story, but Gray Feather spoke first. "There are stories of such creatures in this country too," he said. "Old stories, passed down over the years. But those animals are all gone now . . . or so I thought."

"What kind of animals?" Conner asked.

"Oh, giant crocodiles, huge bearlike creatures, great ground-thumpers whose descriptions sound to me an awful lot like a mix between an elephant and a buffalo. I have not personally seen any of these things, but stories persist that a few of the ground-thumpers might still be around."

Kit said, "Even if any of these . . . these ground-thumpers did exist, and one happened to be alive and roaming these mountains, from what you say, it should have left tracks that went deep, all the way to solid ground."

"You would think so," Gray Feather agreed.

"Not if it was a beast from the fairy mounds," O'Farrell said very quietly.

They studied him in the fading daylight through the window. O'Farrell went on, "They go their way with hardly a trace. Except for the fairy rings where they danced the night away. For the most part they leave no footprints, no tracks at all. A monster it may be, Mr. Carson, but if it be of the fairy mounds, only the light touch of its feet upon the snow would be left behind."

A chill crept through Kit as O'Farrell's wide gaze reflected the firelight. Everyone felt it.

All at once Bodine emitted a cry of terror.

Kit wheeled about to see what was wrong, fearing it was something to do with the surgery.

But it wasn't the operation. Bodine was staring out the window, pointing, his mouth opening and closing, but no words coming out of it.

Chapter Six

"Saints protect us! We're camping on haunted grounds!" O'Farrell declared, moaning and holding his head, shaking it back and forth.

"Enough of that, Sean!" Kit ordered as he and Conner tried to calm Bodine.

"Tell us it again, slower this time," Conner said, gripping the terrified man's shoulders "What was it you saw?"

Gray Feather had grabbed up a rifle and was peering past the corner of the blanket that they had dropped back down to cover the opening in the wall. "I don't see anything out there now, Kit," he said, scanning the lengthening shadows that crawled across the valley now that the sun had dipped behind the mountain peaks.

Bodine got a grip on himself, then managed a grin as he rested his head back on the saddle. "It's that

Irishman and his crazy tales. Fairy mounds. Monsters. Winged serpents. It's got me spooked."

"You saw something. What was it?" Kit urged, having his own reasons for wanting to know.

Bodine's eyes shifted to Kit's face. "I couldn't have seen anything, Kit. Leastwise, not what I first imagined."

"Most likely not, but tell me anyway."

"Well, I was listening to O'Farrell talking about those monster critters they have back in Ireland, about those flashing scales. And right about then a flash of light out the window caught my eye. I looked. There was another flash . . . then I saw this . . . this thing walking on two legs, like a man, only it wasn't a man—couldn't have been a man." Bodine laughed. "Think I've gone crazy, don't you?"

"What makes you think it can't be a man?" Kit asked.

"Well, it went on two legs all right, but every time it moved it's skin would catch the sunlight going down behind that peak out there. But there was something else, too. Instead of a head, it had this . . . this thing. I can't describe it."

"Might a rack of elk antlers describe it, with long hair flowing behind them?"

Bodine's eyes rounded. "That's exactly what it was! Antlers, or something that looked very nearly like antlers."

Kit sat back.

"You know what it is?" Gray Feather asked.

"No, but I've seen Bodine's monster too. Last night. Something woke me and I went out to check on the horses, thinking we might have a cougar prowling about. That's when I saw it."

"Oh, no," O'Farrell groaned, shrinking into the corner and shaking his head. "This is the work of the fairy folk for sure. They are coming after me!"

"After you?"

"Aye, Mr. Carson. They be family spirits, like I already told you. It is why I fled Erin years ago. They came to take away me father and me uncle, and now they followed me here. There be no ocean so wide a fairy folk can't find their way across it, to be sure."

"No one is coming to take you away," Kit said, moving to the window and lifting a corner of the blanket. Night had completely enveloped the land. There were a few gathering clouds in the dark sky, and a wind had begun to blow. But other than the rattling of tree limbs and their shadows dancing against the fields of snow, nothing else moved.

"There are no fairy monsters out there," Kit said, turning back to O'Farrell. "Whatever it is, it's real, and I'll prove it. Tomorrow I'm gonna track the critter down and bring it back."

O'Farrell shook his head, a strange light in his stretched eyes. "No, you'll never do it. You can't catch the fairy folk. No one can. They're not like the wee folk. They can't be caught, can't be killed. The banshee, she's one, and there's nothing you can do to stop her when she comes for you."

At that moment a gust of wind wailed softly through the chinks in the logs. O'Farrell leapt where he sat and his fist tightened around one of the hearthstones, his quick glances darting about the cramped cabin.

Bodine had begun to moan again, squeezing his eyes shut against the pain.

Kit shook his head. It was going to be a long night.

No one talked about ghosts or Wendigos or mountain demons that night, yet not one man there had a good night's sleep. O'Farrell, for his part, spent hours huddled near the fire, his knees drawn to his chest and clutched about by his arms. Finally, about four in the morning, steady breathing began coming from O'Farrell's corner. Thomas Conner dozed on and off, waking often to check on Andy Bodine. Bodine was moaning worse than O'Farrell's banshees. It was this constant, soft, breathy torment that kept Kit awake. This, and Conner's and his effort to fight Bodine's fever with damp cloths. And something else, too. Throughout the night Kit's ears had remained tuned to the sighing wind, sifting it for any sounds that didn't belong there. But the night passed without incident. The horses had kept quiet, and no mysterious bumps or distant wails intruded on them. Although he had gotten little sleep, Kit welcomed the first hint of morning that crawled across the sky.

As dawn broke full upon the mountainside, Andy Bodine finally fell into a deep, restful sleep. Sleep was what the injured man needed most, and the trappers were careful not to wake him as they went about the business of boiling coffee and gnawing strips of jerked venison and eating what was left of the rabbits O'Farrell had killed earlier.

"I'll be wanting to see those tracks this morning, Mr. Carson. And that dead Indian," O'Farrell whispered after they had eaten. With the daylight, the Irishman had regained much of his bravado.

"I wouldn't mind going along too," Gray Feather said.

"I'd want to take a gander at that Indian myself," Conner put in. "Ain't never seen one of them burial scaffolds yet."

They had all been cooped up too long. With a bright sun in a clear sky warming the frozen land, everyone was anxious to get out and stretch their legs. Bodine was still sleeping soundly, and from the looks of it, would stay that way for several hours.

"It's not far. Reckon it wouldn't hurt to leave Andy here alone for a few minutes while we take us a trek over thar," Kit decided.

The three of them crawled quietly out the door. Kit paused and looked back at the sleeping man. Bodine was breathing evenly, shallowly. The cabin was warm, and they had left a fire burning to keep it that way. Carefully, he lowered the blanket and anchored it in place.

They followed the tracks Kit had made the day before. The forest soon closed in around them, and in a minute the cabin was lost to view, although the smoke from its chimney could still be seen and smelled. When they came to the strange tracks, O'Farrell stared at them without speaking.

Gray Feather measured the stride and frowned. "These can't be animal tracks, Kit."

Kit nodded. "You can bet that whatever made them, it couldn't have been one of them ground-thumpers."

"But what about the creature's strange appearance, Mr. Carson?" O'Farrell asked. "You saw it, and so did

Mr. Bodine. It had antlers growing out of its head. And the shape of these tracks. There be nothing I know of that leaves a shape like this."

"I only caught a glimpse of the critter. And that's all Andy saw, too. And both times, the light was poor. It could have been anything."

Today the tracks were even fainter than when he had first come across them. By now the only thing that he could judge for a certainty was their size; blowing snow had obscured the details.

"Aye, it could have been *anything*. But methinks it mighty strange this creature shows up here, on the very ground where a dead man lays."

"You have got to be the most superstitious man alive," Conner scoffed.

"There might be some truth in what he says," Gray Feather allowed.

Kit looked surprised. "Don't tell me a man with all your schooling believes in this?"

"I've heard the stories that my people have told of such things, Kit. There is not a Ute alive who will tell you that ghosts aren't real."

Kit had ridden with Gray Feather several years now, but this was the first time he had heard the half-breed speak of such things.

"Aye! And I'll wager Mr. Feather knows a thing or two about these mountain demons, him being born and raised here and all." O'Farrell backed away from the tracks and stared into the forest, turning a slow, careful circle. "It be out there somewhere—somewhere nearby. Just watching us."

Conner shook his head. "Well, these old tracks

aren't telling us much. We need to find us some fresh prints that haven't been filled in with snow. Where's that dead Indian?"

Kit pointed with his rifle. "Just this way a couple hundred feet. Come on, boys, and take a gander."

They trekked through the deep snow. It was slow going, but the distance wasn't great and five minutes brought them to the clearing, gathered around the scaffold, peering at the blanket-covered shape lying there. A cold wind had begun to wend its way through the clearing and ruffle the fur of their coats. It had started when they entered the clearing, and O'Farrell shivered and looked over his shoulder again as if the wind was the icy fingers of death.

"I don't like this place," the Irishman said, his eyes rounding. "I think we best be going now."

Conner poked at the blanket with the barrel of his rifle. "Frozen solid."

"Now, you best not be doing that, Mr. Conner," O'Farrell said worriedly.

Conner laughed. "Why? Think that frozen Injun is going to sit up and give me a piece of his mind?"

"It's not respectful to the dead," Gray Feather said.

"Aye. And you don't want to be stirring up the wrath of the spirits against us," O'Farrell added, looking over his shoulder again.

"Now, that's strange," Kit said, moving closer to the scaffold.

"What?" O'Farrell asked, a little too quickly.

"Whal, I put Bodine's leg right thar, right next to the Injun. But it's gone now." Kit brushed some of the snow from the burial scaffold to be sure.

"Gone?" O'Farrell inched closer and looked for himself.

"An animal must have taken it," Gray Feather said.

"Maybe." Kit looked down at the snow, well trampled now by the men standing around it. Something caught his eye. "I think I found what took it."

They each peered long and hard at the huge footprints that led away from the scaffold.

"Saints protect us!"

"That's a pretty clear track, Kit," Conner said softly.

"Clear enough to follow," Kit answered.

"You aren't thinking of tracking that demon!" O'Farrell declared.

"You can go back to the cabin if you want."

O'Farrell didn't know which way he wanted to go. Finally he said, "I think we best stick together."

Gray Feather said, "It's got my curiosity up. I'll tag along with you for a piece, Kit."

Kit didn't think Bodine would awake anytime soon, and they had been away only ten minutes. Not even enough time for the fire to burn itself down. But he didn't want to be away too long. "We'll just follow them a little way and see what direction they take off in. Then we'll go back to the cabin and see how Bodine's doing."

The tracks led off to the north, and it took Kit only a moment to realize that whatever had made them had been man-size, and not a very big man at that. The stride was easily human length, and the only explanation for the huge footprints was that the man who made them must have been wearing snowshoes of some curious design.

After only a few minutes the tracks became confused as dozens of different trails either came together or led off in different directions. One trail caught his eye. All the others seemed to branch off from it. The trace led them to a sheer rock face and a steep ledge that angled up it.

On this narrow rim of rock most of the snow had been swept clean by the hard winds that blew across the exposed shelf. The forest fell quickly away beneath the trappers as they climbed higher, and soon a vast ocean of treetops spread out below them. Kit's ears were tuned for any sounds from ahead, while his sharp eyes took in every detail of the trace. Whoever came this way had done so many times before. What little dirt had collected upon the shelf, and the sparse grasses that had grown there that summer, were trampled flat. Here and there something had gouged deep indentations in it, while other places showed the rounded impressions of a moccasined foot. Oddly, at regular intervals Kit detected a small, deep impression accompanying each print. As if a walking stick was being used.

When the ledge took a sharp turn, Kit brought the men behind him to a quiet halt. Putting a finger to his lips, he silently indicated they should wait there for him while he went ahead. Easing forward, the mountain man sidled against cold rock and pushed his head around the edge of a slab of iced granite. The narrow trace ended just beyond, widening a bit to about ten feet. A dark shadow slashed across the face of the rock there, blacker than a shadow ought to be. Kit's eyes narrowed against the glare. It was more than a shadow. It was the mouth of a cave.

After giving a signal to the others to wait, Kit moved out in a crouch and drew up against the rock, listening for movement from inside. He heard nothing except the constant rush of wind sweeping down along the rocky precipice and the drumming of his heartbeat in his ears. Kit sucked in a breath, held it, and lurched into the cave, swinging his rifle side to side.

The cave was empty. Kit's view darted in and out of the deeper shadows, but nothing moved; no lurking dangers leaped out at him. Straightening up out of the crouch, he let go of his breath. The rear of the cave went deeper than the daylight could penetrate. What lay hidden within its depths he could not know. He listened. Nothing. Against the far wall, out of the way of the cave's mouth, blackened stones had been fashioned into a ring upon the dusty floor. Next to them was a pile of firewood. The acrid smell of smoldering wood filled the place. A blanket was spread out upon a pallet of pine boughs, and nearby it was a small, woven basket decorated in symbols of some kind. It was too dark for Kit to make them out.

Kit went to the fire ring. The rocks still held the warmth of a recent fire. A pit had been dug inside the circle, filled with ashes and glowing embers. Whoever had built it intended to come back. He stuck his head outside and called the men forward.

They poked around a little bit, then came back to the ring of the hot stones. The mouth of the cave faced southwest. Come noon, and throughout the latter half of the day, sunlight would fill and warm it, but right now it was dark and cold.

"What do you reckon this place is?" O'Farrell asked quietly, looking about.

"Someone is using it for a lodge, from the looks of it," Gray Feather said, examining the basket. Inside it were scraps of meat and gnawed bones.

"Someone? Or some*thing*?" O'Farrell pressed his back against the dark wall, his rifle ready.

"Kit, take a look at this," Gray Feather said. "I can't be sure, but from the markings, I'd say this was Blackfoot."

The basket had lived well beyond its usefulness and was badly frayed and coming apart at the seams. "Could be," Kit said. "And it could be that it was stolen."

"Can I see?" Conner asked.

Kit handed it to the young man and went back to examining as much of the cave as the outside light would permit. The blanket was a Hudson's Bay Company point blanket, as badly worn as the basket.

Conner set the basket down, then stopped suddenly, staring at something on the floor. "Kit!"

Kit's glance followed Conner's pointing finger.

"My God," O'Farrell moaned.

It was Bodine's amputated leg. The meat of it, above the gangrene, up around the knee joint, had been cooked and then gnawed away from the bone.

"Saints protect us! There be a demon here!"

Kit's stomach took a couple of turns before settling down. No one seemed able to speak for a few moments.

"I think we better leave this place," Conner murmured finally.

"Might be a good idea," Kit agreed. They had been jumpy to begin with, and the sight of the gnawed leg was almost more than anyone could take and remain completely calm. O'Farrell's grip had frozen tight about his rifle, and Kit feared at the least provocation he might let loose a shot, and in his condition that could be dangerous for all of them.

They were about to leave when two rows of markings upon the wall, where the line between dark and daylight met, caught Kit's eye. He crossed the dusty floor, squinted at them in the faint light, and said, "What do you make of these, Gray Feather?"

The Ute studied them a moment, frowning, then shook his head. "Can't make them out, Kit. But they seem to be symbols of some kind. Or maybe only the meaningless scribblings of an idle mind."

Conner peered at them, his mouth slowly working its way into a tight, thoughtful knot. "There was a child back where I growed up who was simple in the head. She used to scratch in the dirt with a pointed stick all the time, and what she drew looked something like this."

O'Farrell worked his way over and glanced at them. "No!" he cried.

"What is it?" Kit asked, seeing the Irishman's face blanch and his eyes stretch.

He stammered, then said, "You know what those are?"

They had to wait for O'Farrell to settle down. His voice was suddenly whisper-quiet, and his view darted toward the dark unknown at the back of the cave. "They be the secret writings of the wee folk—the elfin demons' runes!" He took a step backward, then another, and suddenly turned and rushed out of the cave.

Kit, Gray Feather, and Conner looked at one another. Before anyone could speak, the distant report of a pistol shot reached them from the valley below.

"Bodine!" Kit said, springing out of the cave a half-dozen steps behind the terrified Irishman.

Chapter Seven

Andy Bodine swung the pistol, leveling it at the doorway, when Kit pushed his way through. Sweat poured down Bodine's face, and a wild look of terror was in his eyes. For an instant Kit feared for his life. Then Bodine realized who it was. He dropped the pistol to his chest and lowered his head back to the saddle. "It's you," he breathed, blinking and licking parched lips. "Thank God it's you, Kit," he said.

Kit moved all the way inside, and the others came through the low door behind him. "What happened?" The odor of gun smoke was thick in the air. A second pistol lay at Bodine's side.

"It came for me, Kit. That monster. It came," Bodine said.

"What was it that come for you?" O'Farrell asked softly.

Bodine's wide eyes came around. "It was a monster,

I tell you. It was at that window watching . . . just watching. I could feel its eyes peering in on me. I . . . I must have been half asleep, then suddenly I was full awake, but I didn't open my eyes right away. I just lay here, listening, hearing its breath, smelling its stink. I could stand it no longer. I was about crazy with fear. I opened my eyes and saw it. It was coming through the window! All I could think was to get my hand on a gun. I grabbed up a pistol, but it was already retreating by the time I could get off a shot."

"Did you hit it?"

Slowly his head rolled from side to side. "I don't think so. It was already out the window. And I couldn't move to take my second shot." He stopped, licking his lips, his Adam's apple bobbing. "No, I don't think I hit it, Kit."

"Saints protect us!" O'Farrell lamented, staggering back against the wall of the cabin and slipping to the ground like a rag doll. "Now it's coming after us!"

Kit went outside and found the fresh tracks outside the window, just as Bodine had claimed. Whatever it was, it was long gone. Its trail swept past the horse corral and bent back around into the forest. Searching high and low, Kit did not find a hint of blood anywhere on the unspoiled snow.

"There would be no blood, Mr. Carson," O'Farrell interjected into Kit's report. "Ghosts don't bleed!"

"I didn't think I hit it," Bodine murmured. He'd calmed down and regained control of himself.

"What did you see, exactly?"

"Just like I saw yesterday. I'd swear it's like nothing I've ever seen before. It has antlers, like an elk, but the

91

face! The face was . . . was . . . " Bodine looked Kit in the eye with the pitiful expression of a man questioning his own sanity. "The face was that of a skeleton. No skin on it, only bone, and two empty eye sockets staring in at me."

O'Farrell moaned and clutched his head in his hands. "It be that mountain demon come to have us! We're camped on haunted ground, we are." Suddenly his head snapped up, his eyes big as walnuts. "It's the ghost of that dead Indian, that's what it is!"

"Sean, put a cork in it it," Kit snapped. All this talk of demons, ghosts, and wee folk was getting to him too, and discovering Bodine's half-eaten leg back in the cave hadn't helped matters. "I don't know what it is roaming around out there, but it's *not* a ghost!"

"And how can you say so with such plum sureness, I ask you?"

Kit snorted his disgust and said, "I'll tell you how I can say so. I've never yet heard of a ghost that needs to eat, or to cook its food, for that matter."

That stunned O'Farrell into a sort of thoughtfulness as he leaned back against the wall to consider Kit's words. Kit was careful not to say anymore than that, and he suspected the others felt as he did. Bodine did not need to hear the grisly details of what they had discovered.

Bodine licked his lips. "I could use a chaw about now. Can one of you coons pass me my bag over there?"

Gray Feather lifted the man's possibles bag off its peg and gave it to Bodine. Bodine rummaged through it, removing items before finding a quarter carrot of tobacco wrapped in brown linen. Among the possessions that he had piled on the ground next to him was the little, longhaired, buckskin-clad doll that had started this whole disastrous episode.

Bodine paused, holding it. He smiled briefly, but the momentary glow swiftly faded and he shoved it back into the bag along with a brass bullet mold and a spare tin of percussion caps.

No one spoke at first, especially O'Farrell, who appeared caught up in his own thoughts. Then Conner said softly, "Andy, I seen the look in your eye just now. What is it?"

Bodine blinked a couple times, managing a small grin. Sunlight through the window glistened in his eyes. "You mean little Princes Waterfall?"

"Maybe I shouldn't have mentioned it. None of my business anyway," Conner went on quickly, hearing the emotion squeeze Bodine's throat.

Bodine held the little doll in both his hands, peering at it. "Reckon it's because of her that you . . . me . . . all of us are here right now." He glanced at O'Farrell, but the Irishman was staring at the dirt beneath his moccasins.

Although O'Farrell pretended not to be interested, Kit caught the twitch at the corner of his mouth and a tick in his left eye. The Irishman was listening, all right, in spite of his pretensions.

"Reckon that sort of makes it your business now, Tom. Yours and everyone else's." Bodine speared O'Farrell with a quick glance, then went on. "I know you think it strange, and maybe it is, a full-growed man hanging on to to something like this."

"We figured you had your reasons," Kit said.

Bodine looked at the doll, but he was clearly seeing something else. "She was only eight years old," he began slowly. "She had only just had her birthday the week before . . . before the fire. Her mama, Evelynne, had spent almost a month making this doll, sewing on it in the evenings by lantern light, after her work was done and Melissa was asleep in her bed. You would've had to have been there, watching and listening, to understand the love that went into making little Princess Waterfall—that's what Melissa named her."

He sat there with a twist of tobacco in one hand, the doll in the other, thinking, remembering. "I was over to Butler Creek, taking a load of corn and potatoes to trade for a new ax head and some calico Evelynne had seen when we had been in a few months earlier. I wasn't home when it started. Ben Horsely, he met me on the road on my way back to tell me what had happened. Said he'd seen the flames light up the night sky clear over at his place, across the hollow. He had come over right away, him and his two sons, Hobey Joe and Toby, but it was too late.

"Never did know what started it. When I got there nothing was left of the place. Later, after the timbers cooled enough for me to look for them, I . . . I . . . " His words caught in his throat. "I found Evelynne and Melissa huddled together in a corner, behind a piece of the ceiling that had come down. Wasn't hardly enough to bury, but I did, out behind where my father and his brother lay. I dug the hole and laid them together, next to Peter." He looked up from the doll. "Peter, he was our firstborn, but he died of a fever when he was but two years old.

"Afterward, I was standing there looking at the charred ruins of my life, wondering how it would ever be all put back together again, not really thinking, just staring. That's when I happened to spy Princess Waterfall sitting on the top fence rail, leaning against the post." He gave a short laugh, but there was only sorrow in it. "Melissa must have left her there after playing. It was all I had left—all that I could touch, hold, at least. I still have a head full of memories."

Bodine's fist tightened about the doll, and suddenly there was anger in his face. "And look where it's gotten me! I wish it had burned up in the house with everything else." He thrust the doll back into his bag and bit a chunk of tobacco off the carrot, working it fiercely between his teeth.

"I didn't know you ever had a family," Conner said quietly.

"I don't talk about it."

"That why you come out to the mountain?" Kit asked.

"Reckon there wasn't nothing left for me back in Kentuck. I seen an advertisement for work on the wharves at St. Louis, so in '28 I made my way there. With all the new steam power travel, the river had become a mighty busy place and there was lots of work. That next spring I happened to meet William Sublette. He had come in from the wilderness to make up his supplies and hire men to go west and trap for his Rocky Mountain Fur Company. I had no particular direction left in my life and the West looked as good as any other, so I joined up with Sublette. In March of '29 sixty of us *mangeur de lard*, along with our mules and horses packed heavy with Captain Sublette's provisions, left Missouri and pointed our noses west. And I ain't been back since."

Bodine worked a wad of tobacco into his cheek and glanced around. Kit passed him a tin cup to serve as a temporary cuspidor.

Silence filled the cabin. Bodine chewed and spit. Gray Feather frowned thoughtfully, his thumb absently stroking the raised embossment of his book of Shakespeare. Conner glanced at Kit, but neither man had anything to say. The only one there who should have had something to say was O'Farrell, and he wasn't talking. But Kit thought the Irishman looked mighty uneasy over by the fireplace—a little like a woebegone castoff sitting atop an ant hill, fidgeting and scratching a furrow in the dirt floor with the edge of his moccasin, being particularly careful not to accidentally catch anyone's eye.

Kit looked out the window, then leaped to his feet and pointed out it. "Will you boys come and look at this!"

They crowded about the window, Bodine craning his neck where he lay, asking what it was.

Kit let out a whoop and said, "There will be hump ribs and boudins today."

"Buffalo?"

Kit said, "Give way so as Andy can see!"

Bodine levered himself up on his elbows and gawked at the moving landscape down in the valley below the cabin. It was all brown and black and shaggy, and sunlight glanced and danced off a sea of shiny black horns. Kit was already reaching for his coat and hat.

"I'll go with you," Gray Feather declared, excited as a boy on his first hunt.

Kit grabbed his buffalo rifle, a well-used, full-stocked J. J. Henry, built after the Lancaster pattern. The smokepole was a heavy .32-gauge shoulder thumper that was as much an extension of Kit as was his own arm and hand.

"Come along, Sean," Kit said.

"Me?" The Irishman seemed surprised to have been invited.

"It'll do you good to get out of this place for a spell."

The funk lifted from the man's face like fog burned off by a morning sun. In the long scheme of things, O'Farrell might have been the one to blame for Bodine storming out in anger, resulting in his travail now, but which man among this hardy, raw-boned breed of mountaineers had not gone overboard a mite on his teasing—all except for Jim Bridger, Kit mused, whose chronic bouts with sobriety were renowned throughout trapper camps far and wide? These Shining Mountains were full of the graves of men who were there because someone's practical joke or thoughtless remark had gone calamitously awry. Kit was not one to hold O'Farrell's feet to the fire on account of past sins.

"They're moving down to lower ground, looking for open grass," Kit told Bodine.

"There must be over two hundred of 'em." Bodine dragged himself over to see better, wincing at the pain it caused him. The herd was moving slowly but steadily through the deep snow. By the time the men were in their coats, hats, and gloves, and had their rifles ready, the tail end of the migration had already moved past the cabin's line of sight.

"I'll stay with Andy," Conner said, and made way for the men to clamber out the small doorway.

"You do that. We'll be back directly with victuals for these weary meat bags of ours. Build us a good fire, for we feast tonight!" Kit declared just before the blanket fell back in place.

They dug their saddles out of two feet of snow where they had cached them beneath a canvas covering. Their horses were feisty and full of energy, straining at their halters as the men saddled and cinched. They, like the men, were in need of diversion and some exercise after enduring days of captivity.

The sun was warm, but the air was still colder than a pile of dead man's bones. Kit gave a wry smile, wondering what had caused him to think of that. Giving a hoot just for the pure joy of it, Kit led the way out of the corral. It was slow going until the horses had kicked a fresh trail down into the valley. Coming upon the trampled snow left behind by the migrating herd, the horses kick up their hind legs and jogged along spry as carefree yearlings.

Soon they had the buffalo in sight. From a distance the herd could have passed for a shadow moving across the land. It wasn't but a few minutes before the riders were swinging wide to come up onto their flanks. Urging their horses on, the trappers sawed away at the virgin snow, fighting their way ahead of the herd, which had yet to sense danger in their presence. Not that it would have done any good if they had. The snow would have stopped any stampede almost as soon as it had started.

Kit turned his horse into the herd and snugged the rifle into his shoulder. When he was still a hundred yards away, his first shot boomed across the snow. One of the animals scrambled forward a few dozen steps, staggered, then lurched forward into the snow.

Kit reloaded as the horse drove on. Gray Feather cut to the left, reins wrapped about the saddle horn. The Ute took aim. The report of his rifle was followed by O'Farrell's shot, echoing across the valley. The herd had begun to run, but as Kit had suspected, the snow hauled them back. Kit fired again.

The trappers' shots rang out like intruders in the cold, still air, stealing the peacefulness from the winter silence. The herd could do little more than turn their shaggy backs on them and plow away through the snow as quickly as they could. When the men drew to a halt and looked back, a string of animals lay behind them, and around each a crimson stain smudged the crisp clean snow.

Some were still kicking at the snow. The hunters dispatched these with their pistols and set about the task of removing the delicacies: the hump meat, tongues, and intestines. Afterward, they skinned the buffalo, draping the valuable hides across each horse and tying them behind their saddles. Finally the men sawed away as many thick roasts as they were able to carry back with them.

By the time they had finished skinning and butchering, a pale, dying sun hung low in the sky. The job had taken hours, although to Kit it seemed as if only a tenth that time had passed. With the approaching dusk, the temperature had begun to plunge again. The meat they were leaving behind would be frozen solid by morning, and would feed the local clawed, furred, and feathered population for days, if not weeks, to come.

Leaving the killing grounds behind, the men headed for home.

The long, thin column of smoke threading skyward from the short chimney was a welcome sight to the cold hunters. Gray Feather put the horses in the corral and fed them cottonwood bark while Kit and O'Farrell tied the meat and furs into a bundle at the end of a long rope and ran them up a tree, out of the reach of animals. They carried in enough hump meat, tongue, and intestine to cook up that night.

Although his pain was mighty, Bodine was bearing up. Conner told them that Andy was looking better. Kit couldn't see it, and he reckoned the young trapper had said that for Bodine's benefit. Best he could judge, Andy was looking no worse. The injured man did his best to keep up his humor, in spite of the terrible agony he was enduring. Trying, Kit supposed, to be no more burden upon them than necessary.

They cooked up the meat and boiled coffee and ate a hearty supper. After the fright Andy had had in the morning, the rest of the day had passed without incident. When their stomachs were full and they were contented and sleepy, Kit said, "If this weather holds, and if Andy looks up to it, we might try to leave this place the day after tomorrow."

Everyone was for the suggestion. Andy said he was

willing to give it a try, as he did not relish another visit from that creature.

"I'll cut us some straight poles and start to work on the travois in the morning," Conner offered.

O'Farrell declared that the sooner they were off this haunted ground, the better they would all be.

There was general agreement on that point, and they threw more wood on the fire. As the cabin warmed and the fatigue of the last several days caught up with them, the men bundled themselves in their furs and drifted off to sleep.

And it would have been a good, restful sleep, too, if the horses had not awakened them in the early hours of the morning.

Chapter Eight

"Kit . . . Kit . . . "

The gentle shaking brought the trapper out of a deep sleep. Instantly he was awake. A man who spends very many years in the wilderness learns he can't afford the luxury of waking slowly. A few seconds could mean the difference between life and death, and those who did not learn the lesson did not live long.

Instinctively, Kit's fist wrapped around the pistol beneath his buffalo-skin coat. Then he saw it was only Thomas Conner. The fire had gone out some hours earlier, and it was black as sin inside the cabin, except for the embers' faint reddish glow.

"What is it?" Kit asked, then stopped, listening. "The horses?"

"Their whinnying woke me about ten minutes ago," Conner whispered so as not to wake the others. "They sound mighty nervous. I was about to go out and take a look, but I wanted someone to know."

Kit saw then that Conner was already bundled into his coat with his hat pulled down low over his eyes.

"Maybe I ought to go with you," Kit said, sitting up. He lifted a corner of the blanket and looked out the window.

"No need. I'm taking my rifle."

Kit nodded. "All right, but if you run into trouble, sing out and I'll be hot on your heels."

"Might only be a cat," Conner said hopefully, but Kit knew what he was really thinking. "Can't afford to lose any horses to a hungry panther."

"Probably that's all it is. Keep your eyes peeled, Tom. A painter can get right brave when it's hungry. This weather brings out the worst in them."

"I will. Be back in a few minutes." Conner slipped out the door and was gone. Kit turned to the window and watched his shadowy form high-stepping through the deep snow toward the corral. The moon was mostly hidden behind a bank of lowering clouds, and there was little light to see by. The storm was moving back in. Kit frowned.

Soft moaning came from a dark corner of the cabin where Bodine lay. Only the shape of him beneath his blankets was visible in the gloom. The cabin was frigid. Kit reached over and stirred the coals with a stick, putting a handful of twigs into them. He puffed the flames to life, arranged a few logs upon them, and had a small fire burning in just a few minutes.

In its flickering light Kit caught Gray Feather watching him, not saying a word.

"Something's got the horses spooked," Kit whispered. "Conner went out to check on them."

The Ute nodded, then pulled his buffalo skin back over his head. O'Farrell turned his face away from the light and resumed his light snoring.

Outside, all remained quiet. Kit moved back to the window. By now Conner was nowhere in sight. The horses had stopped their whinnying and were bunched in the corner of the corral, trying to keep warm. A thin rime of moon glow highlighted the edges of the clouds. Down in the valley Kit thought he saw movement, but when he looked there was nothing there.

A few more minutes passed.

"See him?" Gray Feather asked quietly.

"No. I'm starting to get worried."

"Maybe you ought to go look for him."

"I think this is something he wanted to do alone."

"To prove himself?" Gray Feather asked.

"Something like that."

The Ute was silent a moment, then said, "Comes a time in every man's life when he's got to cut and run on his own. Conner has been with the company since the rendezvous. I know he's still green, but he's toughened up a lot since then."

"I wouldn't be worried except for whatever it is that's out there."

"You don't think it's a ghost?"

"Whatever it is, it's flesh and blood . . . and it cooks its food. There's only one animal I know of that cooks food, writes on cave walls, and uses baskets," Kit said.

Gray Feather nodded. "When you put it like that, it's hard to see it any other way. But who in their right mind would be living in a cave all alone, and moving about on such cold days and nights?"

Who, indeed? Kit wondered. But before he could think that one through, the stillness of the night was ripped apart by the report of Conner's rifle. The reflection of the blast shone orange and red upon the snow beyond the horse corral.

Gray Feather bolted upright.

O'Farrell's eyes snapped open and looked around.

Bodine's groaning came to a sudden halt as the gunshot yanked him from sleep too.

"Conner's found himself trouble!" Kit declared, grabbing up his rifle and coat and diving out the door.

The bitter cold cut through him as he buttoned himself into the heavy buffalo skin on the run. The path through the snow to the corral had been worn deep by their many treks back and forth to tend to the animals. Kit reached the enclosure quickly, then followed Conner's tracks around it toward the rock outcropping on the far side that served as one edge of the corral.

"Tom!" he called, then paused to listen. The wind was picking up. Kit strove on, coming to the wall of granite where he'd seen the reflection.

"Tom!"

The horses milled about nervously, eyeing him with suspicion. "Settle down," he soothed as he gentled the muzzle of one of the horses, looking every which way at once. Something moved among the shadows.

"Tom?"

A dark figure fled across the white ground, moving swiftly in spite of the deep snow. It darted from the shadows and then just as quickly melted into the black-

ness of the forest. Kit was about to follow, but something dark upon the snow near the deeper darkness of
the outcropping's shadow caught his eye. Kit plunged
through the snow, fighting it every step of the way.

Conner was facedown. His rifle lay half buried a
few feet away.

"Tom!"

Kit turned the man over and felt the warm dampness
upon his back. Conner was bleeding heavily. He was
still breathing, but it was shallow, almost impercepti-
ble. Kit hoisted the man into his arms and struggled
back to the cabin.

Kit and O'Farrell made room for them, and Bodine
did his best to scoot out of the way. Kit laid the unconscious man on his stomach, and when they started to
strip off his coat they discovered that one sleeve had
been nearly cut off and hung there only by a bit of
hide. They exchanged their suspicions in guarded
glances that Bodine did not see. Fear crept steadily
across O'Farrell's face. The firelight showed more
blood beneath the coat than Kit had first suspected. His
butcher knife slit open the shirt.

Blood was flowing from two large wounds, about
four inches apart. Something had stabbed deep and
viciously. One had gone into the left lung, the other
slid along the spine, and if it *had* managed to miss the
heart, it was only by a cat's whisker.

Gray Feather soaked a cloth in the pot of tepid water
near the fire and wiped away the blood for a better
look while Kit cast about for something to try to stem
the flow.

"I've never seen the like of this," O'Farrell

breathed, his wide eyes peering over Gray Feather's shoulder. "Could it be the wounds of a pair of claws, Mr. Feather?"

"Even grizzly bears don't have claws this big."

Kit said, "Claws would have ripped his back wide open. Those are punctures. Like a knife or lance might make."

"Or teeth," O'Farrell whispered, his eyes expanding beyond belief.

"Is he going to make it?" Bodine asked, looking worried and helpless upon his pallet.

"I don't know." Kit wished he could have told him more. Andy was struggling against his own pain, and now this. Tom and Andy had become close friends over the course of several months.

Gray Feather put an ear to Conner's back and listened. "Heart's still strong."

"He's lucky that whatever did this missed his pumper." Kit pushed a piece of cotton left over from the amputation into the wound that was bleeding worse.

"Left lung sounds collapsed, too."

Kit grimaced. "No remedy for that I know of. Best we can do is try to stop the bleeding and keep him warm."

Gray Feather searched through his possibles bag and came up with a salve he carried with him. Kit didn't know what it was made from. He'd watched the Ute preparing it a time or two, and each preparation seemed to vary slightly from the last, depending on the items available. He did know that among other things, the salve contained rendered bear grease, plantain leaves, nettles, oil of acorns, and whiskey.

They worked over Conner for the next hour. Finally Kit and Gray Feather stopped the flow of blood, but he'd lost a lot and was pale as a ghost. They wrapped him in his blanket and buffalo robe and kept the fire burning hot, which took all their wood. When Kit asked O'Farrell to collect more, the Irishman refused, claiming the mountain demon was still out there and he wasn't setting foot outside the cabin until daylight.

Daylight, however, was nearly upon them. Rather than cause a row here and now, with two badly injured men confined in the small cabin, Kit shrugged into his heavy coat and shoved two pistols under his belt. "I'll go. Got to collect our rifles anyway. I left them where I found him."

Dawn was in the sky, casting a rosy hue across the snow. The storm clouds of that night had moved off, leaving scattered streaks of dark gray high in the sky. The moon was still visible, but sitting low, quickly sinking into the treetops to the west. Kit retraced his steps around the corral to retrieve the firearms first. When he came to the spot, the rifles were missing. He searched the snow again in case he had overlooked them, but they were gone. Whoever had tried to kill Conner had come back and taken them.

In the growing light he examined the crushed snow where Conner had fallen. It looked to Kit as if the man had been attacked from behind. A sharp blow had shoved him forward into the snow. Whatever was prowling around out here, it had caught Conner by surprise. The rifle shot was probably a reflex action of his finger as he fell. The snow there was stained red with his blood, and all around were the same huge, three-toed prints they had followed to the cave yesterday.

What was it? Who was it? And why did it try to saw off the sleeve of Conner's coat? There could be only one reason. The thing was hungry, and apparently it had a taste for human flesh. Kit shivered at the notion and drew a pistol, turning a slow circle.

Nothing was there.

With the gathering dawn, he spied the ledge in the outcropping. More prints trampled the snow there. Judging by where Conner had fallen, whoever had tried to kill him had been hiding in the dark up on this ledge. Conner likely never knew what had hit him.

But what *had* hit him?

It made no sense, but the more Kit thought about it, the more he was certain the punctures in Conner's back had to have been made by the tines of an antler. . . .

The creature had antlers. Both he and Bodine had seen them. Kit had gotten a glimpse of them again as the creature was fleeing Conner's body. What kind of man-creature had antlers? None that Kit had ever heard tell of from any Indian or mountaineer. What if O'Farrell was right? What if there was some kind of mountain demon critter living hereabouts?

Kit had more questions than answers, and he did not like that. He was determined to get to the bottom of this—and to get their rifles back!

He returned to the corral and gave his horse a hard rub behind the ears. "Wish you could talk," he said to her. "Reckon you saw what it was prowling around here last night. Made you nervous, did it? Wagh! It's giving me the creeps too. About time we track down the 'mountain demon' and see what the critter looks like, huh?"

The horse snorted, and Kit grinned. Leaving it with a final pat, he scoured the area, kicking aside the snow to uncover buried deadfalls, gathering up an armful of wood for their fire. The best that could be done for both Bodine and Conner was to keep them warm and fed. The buffalo hunt had provided plenty of food now, but with all this snow they were chronically short of dry firewood.

Andy Bodine was in a bad way when Kit got back. Not that his amputated leg was acting up more than usual. It wasn't. It was his mood that was giving him fits. He had plunged so low over all that had happened to Conner and to himself that Kit worried he'd take drastic measures. To forestall that, he casually collected the pistols and put them out of his reach. So consumed was he by his despair, the miserable man never noticed.

"Poor Tom," Bodine lamented, peering woefully at his unconscious friend. "This ought not to have happened to him. He had no stake in this. It was all my doing!"

Kit stacked the wood, then hunkered down beside Conner. Gray Feather had placed him upon his stomach with his feet slightly inclined, his head lowered. Every now and then Conner would cough up blood into a rag by his mouth.

"One lung at least is full," Gray Feather said in answer to Kit's unspoken question. "The other sounds clear."

"No way to know if he's still bleeding inside?"

Gray Feather frowned and shook his head. "A doctor might be able to tell you. I can't. But there seems to not be as much blood as before."

"Reckon that's something to hitch our hopes onto," Kit allowed.

"You can't let him die," Bodine moaned, rolling his fevered head. "It's all my fault."

"It's no one's fault," Kit shot back. "No one but that thing out there."

"It's a mountain demon, to be sure. The ghost of that dead Injun, it is. Isn't that right, Mr. Feather? You know of such things!"

To Kit's surprise, Gray Feather did not deny it. The belief in ghosts ran deep and wide through the native peoples of these mountains, and no amount of schooling could ever wipe that particular slate completely clean.

"Enough of that, Sean," Kit said.

"What if he's right?" Bodine said. "What if there *is* something . . . something supernatural prowling about out there?"

"Now, don't you start in on this too. It's a flesh-and-blood thing out thar, and now it's showed itself to be an enemy. Thar's no ghost, and I intend to prove so."

"How?" Gray Feather asked.

"This child is going to run that thing down. I'm of the nature to live and let live, but now that he's tried to kill Tom, time's come to put an end to it. It's no spirit or ghost, Gray Feather. It came back and stole our rifles. What use are guns to a ghost, I ask you?"

"Took the guns?" That surprised Gray Feather, and he had to ponder on it awhile.

"It's hungry," O'Farrell said. "That's why it tried to kill Mr. Conner. It's hungry for the flesh of men. You seen what it did to Mr. Bodine's leg!"

No sooner were the words out of his mouth than O'Farrell realized the slip. He glanced sheepishly at Bodine, stumbled over his tongue a bit, and blurted, "What I really mean to say—"

"What *do* you mean to say?" Bodine asked, looking confused.

"Nothing. I didn't mean nothing. Don't know what I was thinking."

Bodine glared at the Irishman. "What does he mean, Kit?" he said without taking his eyes off of O'Farrell.

"I didn't want to tell you right off, Andy, not with you in such a bad way and flat on your back. But now that Sean let the cat out of the bag, I reckon you ought to know the straight of it. That thing out thar—" he stopped and corrected himself. "I mean that *man*, he went and ate what was left of your leg. He only ate the good meat," Kit went on quickly, "didn't touch the mortified flesh."

Bodine tried to speak, and after a false start or two finally managed to say, "It et my leg!"

Kit nodded.

"You telling me we got us a damned cannibal running around out there someplace?"

"That appears to be the way the stick floats, Andy."

"Good God!" he croaked, staring straight up at the pine-bough ceiling. His eyes shot back, glaring at Kit from a mask of terror that suddenly shaped itself upon his face. "That's why it come back here yesterday when you three were gone!"

"What are you saying, Andy?"

Bodine gulped two or three times. "Don't you see, Kit? It got a little taste of me and now it's coming back for the rest!"

O'Farrell began to moan and groan as if it had been his hide the critter was after.

Kit wondered if there wasn't some truth in what Bodine had said. "We won't leave you alone again, Andy," he promised, but that didn't seem to make the trapper feel much better.

"It et my leg and it tried to eat Tom's arm! That's why his sleeve was cut away. And it will surely come back and finish the job if it can!"

"Andy is right, Mr. Carson," O'Farrell said. "We need to leave this place. Leave right now."

"We can't leave. Not with Andy and Tom in the shape they're in."

Bodine grabbed up the little doll. "Damn this thing! Damn my own sentimentality for holding on to it! If it wasn't for this I'd still have my leg and poor Tom wouldn't have almost gotten himself killed by that thing out there. It's all on account of this doll! I should have buried it with Melissa, where it belonged!"

Crushing it in his fist, Bodine suddenly flung the doll out the window, then turned his head away and buried his face in his arm.

Chapter Nine

Gray Feather had said nothing. He had listened to their heated debate in thoughtful silence, and when finally tempers cooled and a long, uneasy paused ensued, he said, "Maybe it has nothing to do with a taste for human flesh. Maybe whoever's out there doing this is just plain hungry."

"He could have been after one of the horses last night," Kit agreed. "Tom just happened to stumble onto him."

"Sure, and when the fellow got the drop on Tom, he figured cutting off his arm was easier than trying to kill a horse."

Kit grimaced. "A man with no compunctions about eating human flesh over animal flesh has got to be mightily addled in his think box."

Gray Feather gave a short laugh. "That goes without saying."

O'Farrell pulled himself out of his doldrums long enough to ask, "If it is human, how do you explain the antlers, or those empty, ghostly eyes that Mr. Bodine saw?"

That was still a mystery. "I can't . . . not yet, at least. But I intend to find out." Kit glanced back to Conner. The young man had yet to regain consciousness, and his breathing was so shallow that for a moment Kit thought it may have stopped, but then a slight heave of the blanket told otherwise.

"I think of the three of us left, you're the one to stay and look after him and Andy," he said to Gray Feather.

The Indian nodded. "Going back to the cave?"

"That's the first place to look. If he and our rifles aren't thar, then I reckon we'll have to track him."

"Be careful, Kit."

"I'll keep my eyes skinned."

"Want to take my rifle?" the Ute offered.

"With all that's been going on here, you might want to keep it handy." He glanced at the Irishman. "Let's go track us down this man-eating killer."

"Me!" the red-bearded man croaked.

"I don't see anyone else here hale and hearty enough to do it." Kit shoved a pistol under his belt and dropped a second one into the pocket of his coat.

"Maybe I should stay here and help Mr. Feather?"

Kit frowned. "Whal, maybe you should, after all. Won't that make for a good story to tell once we get back to winter quarters? I reckon the men will get a bellyful of chuckles out of it when they hear how being scared of a ghost kept you huddled to your knees thar in the corner."

"You calling me a coward?" O'Farrell challenged.

Kit speared him with a narrowed eye. "I haven't . . . yet. But if I walk of this door and you aren't with me, I'm likely to have a change of mind on the matter."

O'Farrell scowled and grabbed his moccasins and socks from near the fire where they had been drying. "I'll be right behind you."

"I'll wait for you outside." Kit ducked under the low door and stepped out into the bright daylight. A squaw wind was blowing from the south and the temperature was warmer than Kit remembered it being in weeks. The storm that had buried the mountains seemed to have finally moved out. If it wasn't for two hurt men inside, and the missing rifles, which would be difficult to replace this side of the summer rendezvous, Kit would have saddled the horses and left right then. Their animals seemed to be enjoying the change in weather too, sticking their noses over the rails and looking at him expectantly.

"Reckon you fellas are right hungry," Kit said, starting toward them. Something in the snow caught his eye. It was the little doll that Andy Bodine had tossed out the window in a fit of emotion and despair. Later, when this was all over, he might regret having discarded it so hastily, considering all the memories tied up in the little cloth, leather, and hair figure. Kit bent for it and dropped it into his coat pocket.

He took the horses down to the stream, broke a hole in the ice, and let them drink, then threw an armful of cottonwood bark into the corral. "You girls make do with this shoddy fare for a mite longer. Won't be many more days and we'll find you some decent fodder to fill your bellies."

Kit turned away and saw O'Farrell waiting for him by the cabin. "Ready?" he asked, coming back.

"Not particularly. Let's get this over with," O'Farrell gruffed.

Kit started off in the direction of the dead Indian, knowing he could easily pick up the trail to the cave from there. O'Farrell followed behind him, not saying a word. At the burial pallet Kit paused to look at the blanket-wrapped figure once more. In spite of the warming air, the body was still frozen solid. O'Farrell hung back, casting a wary eye about the place, looking relieved when they finally moved on.

Next to Indians, the Irish were about the most superstitious people Kit had ever known. He reckoned that was because at least half the inhabitants of Ireland must be ghosts and fairies and the "wee folks," judging from all that he had ever heard about the place. Kit knew many of the stories well-nigh firsthand, from his father, whose own father had been born in Ireland and had come over to this country in the early part of the previous century.

The trappers picked up the strange tracks again. An icy dampness seeped into their footgear as they pushed their way through the deep snow, which was heavier and wetter today. Soon they were standing below the sheer rock face, peering up at the slender ledge trail hugging its side.

"Let's get this over with," O'Farrell whispered.

Worry lines cut deep into his face, and his eyes jumped back and forth as his fist tightened around the stock of his rifle.

Kit took the lead, mounting the ledge and advancing with his back against the cold rock. They worked their way up it until the sharp bend came into sight. Kit slid the pistol from his pocket and held the trigger back as he silently drew the hammer back to full cock.

He listened to a soft scraping sound that came from beyond the bend, then the clatter of pebbles dribbling down the rock face from above. In a single, swift move he crouched around the corner. . . .

Like the first time, no one was there.

They advanced toward the mouth of the cave. Overhead, more pebbles rained down. "Up thar," Kit said, pointing as a fleeting figure in animal skins disappeared among the rocks above them.

O'Farrell craned his neck, but whatever it was, it had already disappeared. "Was it the demon?" he asked, his voice pitched tight as fiddle string.

Kit drew in a long breath and frowned as he lowered his gun. "That was it, all right. He moves faster than lightning among these rocks."

"Probably knows every foot- and handhold by heart."

"Most likely." Kit was amazed at the figure's swiftness. O'Farrell's observation was right on the mark. Whoever was living up here knew the terrain so intimately that it would take more than just stealth to sneak up on him. Kit wished he could have at least gotten a good look at him.

"Well?" O'Farrell asked, searching the near sheer rocky wall looming straight up. "It's long gone by now."

Kit found some tracks at the far end of the ledge, and upon closer inspection discovered another ledge climbing upward and fit only for mountain goats . . . or someone accustomed to rock climbing. "He went this way."

O'Farrell came over. "You don't intend to follow that demon, not along that little rim of rock?"

The cliff fell straight away at the tips of their moccasins, a hundred feet or more, to a boulder-strewn slope where the trees crept near, their tops a green carpet stretching away below them. The view was dizzying, and Kit backed away, shaking his head. "Not this child. He knows when to cut the chase. Appears to me if we're ever going to catch him, we're going to have to figure a way to lure him out of these breaks." Kit peered up at the treacherously slippery rock rising above them.

"Aye. And that might take a bit of doing, Mr. Carson."

Kit went inside the cave. The sun was still not in a favorable place to show much more of it than it had the first time he was here. The far reaches were still cloaked in an impenetrable blackness. But the rock with the writing was illuminated, and Kit discovered new scratching there. There was a row of five stick men. Three were standing and two lying flat.

"Look at this, Sean."

O'Farrell shuffled deeper inside, moving as if each step was an effort. He nervously combed the tangled red beard at his chin with his fingers as he looked over Kit's shoulder. "It's keeping score on us, it is," he said after a moment. "And this here is its tally sheet, I reckon. Those two must be Mr. Bodine and Mr. Conner."

"And the three still standing are you, me, and Gray Feather."

"It be evil workings going on here, I say," O'Farrell whispered, his anxious glances probing the deep shadows and darting around the cave. "I say we best be leaving just as fast as we can, Mr. Carson."

Kit discovered their rifles among some clutter near the fire pit, where a small flame still burned. "Least he left these behind," he said, retrieving them and brushing the dirt from the locks.

"Let's be going," O'Farrell said nervously, starting for the mouth.

Outside there was still no sign of the cave's elusive inhabitant. Kit looked out over the forest's green roof. From this vantage point it would be impossible to sneak up on the cave without being seen. There had to be another way. . . .

Kit remembered Gray Feather's statement.

Maybe it has nothing to do with a taste for human flesh. . . . Maybe whoever's out there doing this is just plain hungry?

Possibly there was more truth in that than Kit had first realized. He glanced back into the cave at the scattering of bones lying about on the dirt floor. They were mostly small—rabbit size, or rat size—and not that many. Certainly not enough to keep a full-grown man well fed. Kit wondered if instead of being after the horses the night Conner had been attacked, could this stalker have simply been after the buffalo meat that had been cached high in a tree?

O'Farrell had already started down the trail. He turned back impatiently, beckoning with his arm. "Well, you coming, Mr. Carson?"

With the first stirrings of a plan taking shape in his brain, Kit hefted the rifles into his arm and followed the Irishman back to the cabin.

"It's worth a try," Gray Feather allowed after thinking it over. "If food is really what's drawing that thing here, it just might work."

"I'll tell you again. You cannot catch a mountain demon any more than you can catch a moonbeam or a rainbow. It just can't be done, and that's all there is to it!"

Kit ignored O'Farrell and studied the white landscape beyond the single window of their cabin. "That one over thar," he said, pointing at a tree standing away from the others. "If we put it thar he'll have to leave cover to get to it. And when he does, we'll have an open shot at him."

"Can't kill a demon with a galena pill," O'Farrell proclaimed flatly.

Kit glanced at Gray Feather and rolled his eyes. They were both getting fed up with O'Farrell's single-minded insistence that what was prowling around the cabin was a demon of some sort. Even Gray Feather, with his Indian upbringing, and the superstitions of his people drummed into his head as a small boy, had finally seen the truth in this matter. Whoever was out there, he was flesh and blood, and more important, he had proven himself to be deadly.

And he had to be stopped!

"Let's get to it now, before nightfall closes in on us," Gray Feather said, standing.

Conner's shallow, spasmodic breathing had not improved—but at least it had not gotten any worse. He had stopped coughing up blood, but that rattling in his chest was just as loud as ever, and that was a big concern. Men have drowned in their own blood before.

Bodine had slowly withdrawn into himself over the hours, becoming brooding and solitary. Now he was staring . . . apparently at nothing in particular . . . just staring. Occasionally he would grimace when a fresh wave of pain washed over him. That was all. Bodine had likened the misery in the raw stump at one point to a hundred bee stings all at once.

For the last hour he had not spoken a single word. He did not even appear to be listening when Kit had lain out his plan to use the buffalo meat to lure the elusive cannibal into the open where he could either be caught or killed. Since the deadly attack upon his friend, Andy Bodine had detached himself from the rest of them, from the world.

"I need to get out of here and stretch my legs anyway," Gray Feather said. "Getting cabin fever. You'll be all right while I'm gone, Andy?"

The troubled man seemed not to have heard and just kept staring.

Gray Feather let it pass. "Conner is beyond any help I can give him," he commented to no one in particular. "He'll either live or die on his own now.

There's nothing more I can do." He looked at O'Farrell. "I'm going to help Kit bait the trap. Keep an eye on things here for me."

"Aye, Mr. Feather. I'll tend to the lads."

O'Farrell was contented as a lizard on a hot rock to stay right where he was for the time being, bare feet propped up on a warm rock. He'd had enough "ghost chasing" for one day.

They climbed into the heavy coats and, taking their rifle with them, headed back out into the cold to set a trap that they hoped their cannibal would find irresistible. Available human flesh naturally being in short supply, Kit had none to bait the trap with, but he suspected that Gray Feather's surmise of the situation was correct: that this was a villain of opportunity, stealing whatever food was conveniently at hand, not a bloodthirsty fiend whose only lust was for the taste of manflesh.

The idea was simple enough. Put out fresh meat where it could be easily found and reached. Do it in a place where someone watching from the cabin's window had a clear view of it, and an open shot. Once the bait was in place, all they had to do was wait. With two badly hurt men who could not be moved, waiting was something they were going to be doing plenty of anyway.

They transferred the entire cache of fresh buffalo meat to the lone tree, hoisted it over a lower limb, and let it dangle about eight feet above the ground. High enough to keep wolves from tearing it apart, but not so lofty that a determined man couldn't fetch it down.

Satisfied with their handiwork, they scoured the area

for more firewood. Dry fuel was hard to come by. They had already scavenged the rare limb of a deadfall thrust up through the snow. Now they had to dig for downed wood, which was fast becoming the only necessity of life in short supply to them. It was easy enough to cut it down green, but green wood burned poorly. Dry timber was available; it just had to be hunted for. Eventually the trappers gathered up enough to see them through the night. With arms full of timber, they returned to the cabin, cold and hungry, and fixed a supper of roasted buffalo tongue and coffee.

When dusk shadowed the land, Kit and Gray Feather took the horses down to water, and chopped enough cottonwood bark to see the animals through the night.

"I'll stand first watch," Gray Feather volunteered after the men had settled in for the night.

Kit didn't argue. It might be a long vigil ahead, and they couldn't afford to let a sleepy eye miss the night prowler when he came . . . if he came. Kit moved a corner of the blanket aside and studied the dangling bait. From this angle the dark meat stood in stark contrast against the snow-covered background. No one could reach it without being seen.

He let the blanket fall back across the window and bent over Conner, gently probing for the slight but reassuring pulse in his neck. The man's condition hadn't improved much since Kit had carried him in early that morning, except for the bleeding, which appeared to have stopped.

"If he makes it through the night, he stands a good chance," Gray Feather noted at seeing Kit's concern.

Kit nodded.

Bodine had finally fallen asleep. That was the best thing for a man in his condition.

O'Farrell was tending the fire, arranging their steaming moccasins, which hung nearby. He looked up from the task and said, "You get some sleep now, Mr. Carson. I'll keep Mr. Feather company a while longer."

There was nothing more Kit could do. "Wake me in about six hours," he told Gray Feather. Taking his buffalo coat to a corner, the weary trapper curled up in it and went to sleep.

Chapter Ten

The crackle of snapping embers and the soft breathing of the men around him pulled Kit suddenly from his sleep. As was his habit, he lay unmoving for a few moments, listening. Only after he had satisfied himself that nothing was out of the ordinary did Kit roll over and shuck off the buffalo skin.

From his place by the window, with his back against the logs, Gray Feather glanced over. The dim flickering of firelight upon his shadowed face revealed the small smile that lifted the corners of his mouth. "Sleep well?"

"What time is it?"

The Ute shrugged. "Late." He peeked past the saddle blanket covering the window, reading the night sky. "Three or four, I make it."

"Should have waked me earlier." Kit left his corner

and silently moved alongside the window to look for himself. The bait was still dangling from its rope where they had left it, apparently untouched.

"You were sleeping so peacefully I didn't want to disturb you. And anyway, I'm not very tired yet. I've been thinking."

"Thinking? What about?"

Gray Feather gave a lame smile and said, "I've been going over *The Merchant of Venice* in my head." He frowned. "I used to know every word of that comedy, all the way from Antonio's very first, 'In sooth, I know not why I am so sad,' clear to Gratiano's final, 'So sore as keeping safe Nerissa's ring.'" He gave a short, quiet laugh and looked embarrassed. "It must be that I've been out here too long, Kit. I seem to have forgotten some of act two."

"No, Gray Feather. Not act two!"

"Yes, act two."

Kit clucked disapprovingly. "Mr. Waldo Gray Feather Smith, I am thunderstruck. Why, what would them schoolmarms back thar at Harvard College say if word of this ever got back to 'em?"

Gray Feather shook his head. "They would probably boot me right out of the alumni association," he said seriously, then cracked a smile.

Kit laughed and inclined his head at the window. "Anything going on out thar?"

"Nothing very interesting. It's been quiet as a graveyard on a Sunday morning. About an hour ago a couple curious wolves followed their noses over for a sniff, and that's all."

"How's Tom doing?"

"Not much change there either. He's started fevering some, but I've been expecting that."

"Hmm. His body's putting up a fight. That's good . . . so long as the fever don't get out of hand." Kit looked at Bodine, whose even breathing was gently lifting and lowering the shaggy buffalo-skin covering. "What about him?"

"Andy lets out a moan every now and again, but he seems to be sleeping well. I checked his stump a little while ago, and it seems to be healing with no sign of mortification."

Kit grunted his approval. "That poultice you concocted is working, then."

"Appears so."

O'Farrell stirred and opened a sleepy eye. "Any sign of it?" he asked groggily.

"Not yet," Kit whispered back.

"Want I should sit up with you and watch?" O'Farrell offered, levering himself onto his elbows, but Kit told him it wasn't necessary. He had just gotten up, and morning wasn't far off. O'Farrell was easily convinced, and two minutes later he was peacefully snoring away.

"Well, reckon I'll try to get some sleep too, now that you're up."

Kit nodded and lifted a corner to look outside again. "If anything happens, you'll be the second person to know."

But nothing ever did happen.

Dawn reddened the sky a couple hours later, herding the night shadows back into their cramped, daytime lairs. Its soft light brightened the cabin.

Bodine's groaning grew louder as sleep left him.

"Morning," Kit said softly so as not to wake Gray Feather or O'Farrell.

Bodine grimaced back his pain and pushed himself up onto his elbows. His tongue racked across dry lips as he looked around, first at Kit, then the sleeping men. Suddenly he remembered Conner.

"How is he?" There was that note of caution that said he was half afraid to know the answer to that.

"Tom's still holding his own, so far."

Kit saw the momentary dread leave Bodine. He lowered himself again to his warm blanket and stared up at the ceiling, working moisture into his parched lips. "Can I have a drink?"

Kit handed him a tin cup filled with snowmelt. Bodine hitched himself up again, managing to drink on his own. He gave a small smile. "Thanks. Think you can help me outside?" His black mood appeared to have lightened some.

Kit got an arm under him and eased him out the small door. After Bodine had taken care of the necessities of life, he brought him back to his sleeping pallet. The ordeal was painful, but Andy managed it without complaint.

The noise woke O'Farrell and Gray Feather. The Irishman sat up, yawned, and cast off his buffalo skin. "Top o' the morning to you, gentlemen," he declared. "You be looking a new man this morning, Mr. Bodine," he said, stirring up the fire. He added more wood from their diminished pile and set about getting coffee to boil.

"Thanks. I'm feeling better."

O'Farrell grinned as if genuinely pleased at the news.

129

Gray Feather checked on Conner.

"He made it through the night," Kit said.

"Breathing seems to have improved some," Gray Feather noted with an ear pressed to the young man's back.

"Why hasn't he come around yet?" Bodine asked.

The Ute shrugged.

"It's the way the body takes care of these things," O'Farrell said. "I know a man back in County Kilkenny who fell off his roof while putting in the new thatch. He landed square on a hay fork and run the tines clear through himself. We carried the poor fellow inside to his bed, figuring he had heard the banshee's call for sure this time. We doctored him best we knew how, us being country folks with no proper medicine, and no surgeon within fifty miles around to tell us how. No one would have given a farthing for old Harley McCormick's chances for living out the day. But he did. He lay upon his bed not blinking an eye for almost a week. Then one morning his eyes popped open and the first words out of his mouth were 'Where's my tankard of ale?'

"After that, Mr. McCormick was up on his feet and about his business as if nothing had happened. Today he's no worse off than before the accident, except for the scars he carries on him. And he shows them off proudly enough whenever he gets too far into his cups, which is almost every Saturday night." O'Farrell shook his head in mild amazement. "It's just the way the body deals with these kinds of bad accidents."

"He's right," Kit said. "Nothing we can do but keep him warm and fed, and wait."

They ate breakfast, and spent the morning watching the bait, but the stalker never showed. O'Farrell declared that the demon knew it was a trap, and Kit was inclined to agree. Bodine wondered if maybe the thing wasn't smarter than they were giving credit.

Three coyotes pawed at the tree trunk and lifted their noses to the meat tied beyond their reach, then, smelling the scent of man nearby, hurried across the frozen crust of the snow.

The morning had grown old and sun was straight overhead when Thomas Conner's sudden groan startled them. His eyes fluttered open, staring unfocused at the saddle blanket beneath him.

"Tom!" Bodine said, gripping the man about his wrist.

Conner blinked, lifted his gaze, but didn't speak. They gathered around him.

"Can you hear me?" Bodine asked.

Conner looked confused, and when he spoke the rasping words came weakly, as if there was not enough breath to push them out. "What happened?"

"You was attacked by that mountain demon thing," O'Farrell told him.

Kit slanted a sharp, impatient glance at the Irishman. O'Farrell frowned and backed off.

"I can't hardly . . . hardly breathe. Someone sitting on my back?"

Kit said, "You got a bad wound to it, Tom. Punched a hole right through one of your lungs."

"Wound? Last thing I remember was checking on the horses. Walked away from . . . corral and turned . . . and . . . and that's all I can remember."

"You were jumped from behind," Kit told him.

"Jumped? Injuns?"

"Don't know yet."

O'Farrell was about to pipe in again, but Kit silenced him with another sharp look.

Conner closed his eyes and appeared to pass out again, but then he looked up at Bodine and said, "How you doing, pard?"

Bodine cracked a small smile. "A far sight better than you are right now. We're both going to have stories to tell soon as we get back to winter quarters. You just gotta work on getting better, Tom. Right soon now we'll be on our way."

Conner gave a quick fleeting grin that evaporated almost at once. His pale face went flat, his eyelids shut, and he was out again, breathing so softly that Kit had to feel for a pulse to reassure himself.

"Well," Gray Feather said.

Bodine released Conner's wrist and lay back, folding an arm over his eyes.

"He'll pull out of it, you'll see," O'Farrell said encouragingly.

Kit wasn't so certain. The Irishman had taken the guilt for both these men upon his shoulders, and Kit wanted to tell O'Farrell that it was not his fault. But before he could frame his thoughts into words, a faint noise reached him from the back side of the cabin. Gray Feather heard it too.

"What do you make of that?" the Ute whispered.

"Something's out thar." Kit reached for a pistol and started for the door.

O'Farrell sniffed the air and said, "I smell something burning."

Kit turned back and listened.

A curl of smoke wove its way through the pine bough ceiling, then another, and with it came the crackle of burning pine needles.

"It's the roof!" Kit dove out the door with Gray Feather on his heels. Flames were leaping skyward from the green boughs and the dry poles that ran the length of the cabin. Plowing through the deep snow, Kit reached the roofline and began dragging off the burning limbs, casting them left and right into the snow.

From inside the cabin came the hacking and coughing of gagging men as smoke billowed from the window and door. O'Farrell appeared at the door first with the unconscious Conner in his arms, fighting his way free of the choking building. Bodine's head popped out right behind him. The injured man was struggling to claw his way free of the deadly smoke.

Kit leaped to Bodine's aid and dragged him out of there. O'Farrell staggered a few paces away and sat down heavily in the snow, drawing the clear air into his lungs in long, rasping gasps, Conner still in his arms.

Gray Feather had finished ripping the burning boughs from the timber frame and was hastily shoveling fistfuls of snow onto the smoldering cross-poles.

Kit dove back inside the smoky cabin for their blankets and coats. They had caught the fire early enough, and upon surveying the damage, Kit found to his relief that only the boughs covering the cabin's roof had burned. The structure under them remained sound enough.

"It could have been a lot worse," he said. "We could have lost everything."

"A death sentence for all of us," Gray Feather noted, glancing at injured men upon the snow, bundled up as best they could be. "Think it was a cinder from the fire?"

Kit prowled around the cabin, looking for signs. He stopped and pointed to a huge track in the snow near the rear of the cabin. "No cinder left these," he said, frowning.

Gray Feather came around and peered at the three-toed tracks leading away from there. "It knew all along what we were up to."

"Looks like this child wasn't so clever after all," Kit replied. He chewed his lip, considering, then shrugged off the failed attempt to catch the prowler in his trap and said, "Whal, we better put the roof back together and get those men out of this cold."

With O'Farrell's help they chopped fresh pine boughs and had the roof patched and the men moved back inside in less than an hour. The wind had swept the cabin free of smoke, and a new fire in the fireplace drove the chill out. Although once again entrenched as snug as before in their bastion against the cold, there was an underlying feeling of apprehension among them now. The close call had shaken them.

Each man understood that their safety depended upon finally putting an end to this threat. There was only one way it was going to be finished . . . and that meant going back to the cave.

That thought made Kit uneasy. He didn't understand why it should. Right then he could not see what it was his subconscious was trying to tell him. It would only be later that he would figure out what it was.

And by then it would be too late. . . .

Chapter Eleven

"He's outsmarted us, the critter has. He'll not take the bait until he's finished with us. This child will wager a season's take on that!" Kit declared.

Gray Feather was nodding. "Setting fire to the cabin was only the beginning. He'll be back."

"It's the very thing a demon would do!" O'Farrell declared. "You cannot fight the mountain demon, ain't that right, Mr. Feather? Your people have tried and failed, haven't they?"

"Legends say he is difficult to kill, not impossible."

"We should be leaving now!"

"Can't leave, Sean. You know that," Kit said. "Jostling Conner on a travois will start his wounds to bleeding again. Can't risk that."

"Instead you're risking all of our lives staying here upon this haunted ground!"

"It's not haunted. And that's not a demon out there.

Whatever it is, it's desperate and hungry, and now determined to be rid of us. But it's flesh and blood, and it can be killed!"

"And how do you propose to do that, Mr. Carson, seeing as we can't catch the thing—or even get a good look at it?"

"I'm not going to wait here until it sets fire to the cabin again. I'm going after it."

"Alone?"

"If I have to. But I wouldn't shun your help, Sean, not if you were to offer it."

Running down the mountain demon was clearly not something the Irishman wanted to do. "You're going to get us both killed," he groused. Then with a frown and a snort he relented. He could hardly refuse to lend a hand without making himself appear a coward before Gray Feather and Bodine. "But I'll go with you."

"I was hoping you would."

The weather was holding. Kit was grateful for that. It appeared the storm had moved out for good, and if history was anything to judge it by, they could expect weeks of fine, springlike temperatures, in spite of it still being midwinter.

It was already late in the day when he and O'Farrell started back to the cave, determined this time to take the critter, whatever it might turn out to be. Although O'Farrell kept quiet on the matter, Kit knew what the Irishman was thinking. O'Farrell felt sure in his heart it was a demon from the netherworld of the dead. Or maybe was one of these wild, hairy men of Indian lore:

137

Skookum, Chiye tanka, T'oylona, Tso'apittse. They went by dozens of names. As Gray Feather had said, each tribe had its own, but they all described the same, huge, hairy, monkeylike creature that supposedly roamed these mountains.

Kit was not inclined to believe in ghosts. But he was open-minded enough to consider that the critter might be one of those strange, hairy, wild men of legend. Stories abounded of such things throughout this country.

But even that was a long shot, and Kit was putting his money on it being a man. A rogue Indian, likely, although he'd not ruled out a renegade white man either. Men living alone in the isolation of these vast uncharted wilds sometimes did crazy things. It wouldn't be the first time these mountains had spawned a cannibal, and it wouldn't be the last, either.

They trudged along in silence, passing by the burial pallet with only a glance in its direction as Kit picked up the now familiar trail that led to the ledge with its cave high up the sheer rock face. Thinking back, he recalled the view from the cave, and how at the time he had thought it would be impossible for anyone to make a frontal approach upon the site without being spotted at once. That was why no one was ever home whenever they came calling. And it would turn out the same today if he didn't change his tactics.

"Where are you going?" O'Farrell asked when Kit suddenly veered off the trail.

"Trying to be sneakier than that critter, Sean. From up thar in his cave, he can spot us a-coming from afar off and skedaddle away before we get near enough to see him—just like he's done before. I don't plan to let that happen this time."

"Aye, sneak up behind the rascal, huh? That's what you be thinking now?"

"I figure if we make for that rocky ground someplace above where his ledge starts, we can skirt its base unseen. If we're lucky, he won't be expecting us from that direction, figuring we'd follow the tracks straight in, like we done the last time. If we can corner him in the cave, we'll have him in our sights."

"*If,*" O'Farrell emphasized. "And it's a mighty big *if,* I be thinking. And I be thinking, too, that maybe cornering that thing might not be such a grand idea. You know what a griz does when he gets his fur up again' a wall."

"We ain't hunting griz."

"Aye, I know," he replied unhappily. "Wish a griz was all we were planning to go up again'."

O'Farrell's superstitions were unshakable. It would take something more than Kit just saying it wasn't so to convince him there was no mountain demon holed up in that little cave.

They broke a fresh trail through the deep snow and in a little while struck upon the rocky escarpment, several hundred yards from where the ledge began its steep climb. Kit was certain they had not been seen this far, yet as he and O'Farrell began their approach that soft warning voice began to whisper at the back of his brain again.

He stopped at one point, not certain why. When O'Farrell cast a questioning eye at him, Kit didn't have an explanation for him, and merely shrugged his shoulders and pushed on.

The afternoon was pleasant, the air warming, and when he breathed, steam no longer burst from his lips like a laboring riverboat. It was the sort of day that might easily loll a man to forget the seriousness of the job ahead. The sunshine, the chirping birds, the clean smell of pine needles were distracting enough, and Kit had to keep pulling his thoughts back around to the reason they were here.

Suddenly a confusion of tracks marred the crisp unbroken snow. The ledge was just ahead, he knew. Sticking close to the rocky wall, the two trappers sidled up to it and paused to survey the rocks around them. Kit eyed the gleaming stretch of land that ran down a gentle slope to meet the nearby forest. Nothing moved out upon that serene, white blanket that covered the land.

Kit could not see far up the ledge. There was only one way to know what, if anything, lay up there. Feeling into the pocket of his coat for his pistol, he discovered something else in there as well.

He had completely forgotten about the doll that he had rescued from the snow where Bodine had flung it. He pulled it out along with the Hawken pistol and gave O'Farrell a wry grin.

O'Farrell only frowned, apparently not seeing the irony in it. If it hadn't been for the doll and for the tender feelings Bodine held for it because of his lost daughter, none of them would be there right now.

Kit could explain it to him later. For now he stuffed the doll away, then checked the cap on the pistol and returned it to the pocket too.

The sun was warm against the rock as they started up the ledge. Kit advanced slowly, alert for the slightest sound that would warn him of what was ahead . . . perhaps just around the bend. When they reached the cave they crept near the mouth and waited, listening. The dripping of melting snow among the warm rocks made a soft plop, plop, plop at the toe of his moccasin. That and the sighing of wind through the treetops below them were the only noises there. Dropping to his haunches, Kit swiftly and silently turned inside the cave, sweeping the dark grotto with the barrel of his rifle.

Once again the cave was empty. Kit was about to stand when his view happened upon a dark form curled up under a blanket upon the sleeping pallet, at the far edge of his view where shadows met daylight. His breath caught in his throat. He could hardly believe his good luck! Signaling O'Farrell to remain behind, Kit inched soundlessly across the dusty floor.

He had the man dead in his sights, and if he had wanted to, he could have killed him right there. Then why was that voice beginning to nag at him again? What was it that set his hairs on end and shot an electric current along his spine? Something was wrong here, very wrong . . . and Kit did not know what it was.

He halted his silent advance and studied the sleeping form. Kit could make out nothing of the man's appearance. He lay half in shadows, with the blanket covering him completely. Not even a head was visible. But the fellow was not nearly as large as Kit had imagined him to be. Up until now he had caught only fleeting glimpses of him fleeing in the night. There were no antlers visible either, and he didn't know if he should be pleased or alarmed by that.

But that wasn't what was nagging him. Then Kit noticed something that had until now escaped him. No matter how soundly a man might sleep, he still breathes. This person was not breathing. The blanket had remained absolutely steady the whole time. Cautiously, Kit stood and nudged the blanket with his rifle. It gave a little under the slight pressure. He tried again, harder this time. There was something under the blanket, all right, but it definitely wasn't flesh and blood!

Suddenly Kit glanced at the place where he had seen the pile of firewood the last time he was here. It was gone. Frowning, he yanked away the blanket, scattering logs and branches and twigs across the floor.

O'Farrell inched up alongside him. "It's the demon's wood supply," he whispered, casting his wary view into the shadowed corners.

"He is not a demon, O'Farrell!" Kit growled angrily. "And he's given us the slip again!" He tossed the blanket aside and looked around the empty cave, at the worn basket of bones near the smoldering fire pit, at the bones of rats and rabbits scattered across the floor, and the scratchings upon the story rock. . . . He looked closer. Something new had been added to it. Next to the stick people they had discovered last time, a rectangular shape had now been scratched into the dark rock. From the top of it was the unmistakable depiction of flames.

"Looky here, Sean."

O'Farrell leaned close to see. "That be the cabin all afire, Mr. Carson. The scoundrel is keeping a tally record on us, it is!"

"Wonder where he is right now?" Kit took a slow turn around the place, his eyes halting on some things leaning against the wall, in shadows. He crossed the small grotto and picked one of them up. "Here's your monster, Sean. Your mountain demon."

"What's that you say?"

Kit tossed a crude snowshoe across to him. "Take a look at that."

"It be the track we discovered in the snow!"

Kit examined the other snowshoe of the pair. It was made of three stout sticks, each two to three inches in diameter, the longest being in the center with the two outriggers arranged in a way that made the snowshoe look more or less like a huge chicken's foot. They were connected with woven strips of bark that served as webbing between the "toes," and in the center of each snowshoe were fasteners to hold it to the owner's feet.

"I say this puts an end to any monsters."

O'Farrell was momentarily speechless. "Then it was a man all along."

"So it appears."

He glanced again at the snowshoe in his hands. "But why did he leave these behind now, Mr. Carson?"

Kit wondered about that himself. Why leave something as useful as these snowshoes unless . . . unless you did not intend to be crossing snow. Snowshoes would be useless to someone planning to climb the tiny ledge he had discovered earlier. Kit's view shot to the scattered firewood, to the blanket that had covered it, neatly arranged to resemble a man. With a sudden twisting in his gut, he knew what it was that had been nagging at him ever since leaving the cabin. He knew why the cabin had been set afire, too, and why they had been able to creep into this cave unchallenged. . . .

"He turned the tables on us, Sean!" Kit cast the snowshoe aside. "He went and set his own trap, and we walked blindly into it!"

O'Farrell's eyes rounded. "Saints protect us!" Dropping the snowshoe he'd been examining, the Irishman leaped for the mouth of the cave.

"Wait!" Kit shouted. If it was a trap, surely it would be sprung as they left the cave.

But the Irishman was in no mind to remain there.

Kit lunged after him, but he was too late. O'Farrell was already out on the ledge. A sound overhead brought them both to a halt. O'Farrell glanced up first.

High above them, among the rocks there, something moved. Kit saw it too: a fleeting glimpse of ragged skins, long, flying hair . . . and a set of antlers standing out sharp and clear against the blue of the sky behind them.

"Out of the way!" O'Farrell cried.

Then the rocks began to cascade down, clattering and cracking like a barrage of gunfire above their heads as they landslided toward the ledge.

O'Farrell dove for Kit and shoved him aside as the first of the rocks came crashing down. A boulder struck Kit's shoulder, another smacked him in the head, and an explosion of blinding lights burst before his eyes. A third rock thumped heavily against his chest, catapulting him back into the cave. It slammed him hard on the floor, driving the breath from his lungs.

Stunned, Kit was vaguely aware of something warm upon his cheek, and there was the taste of iron upon his tongue. He tried to rise but fell back to the floor. His head spun like a top. The cave went out of focus. The last thing he remembered was the cloud of dust billowing in from the ledge beyond.

Then everything went black.

Chapter Twelve

A high-pitched squalling, something like a fiddle string in bad need of tuning, pulled Kit groggily from the cold, black pit of unconsciousness. The annoying noise became an incessant buzzing in his ears. He became aware of a deep ache in his shoulder and throbbing in his head that made him wonder if he had been kicked by a mule. For a long moment he lay with his eyes squeezed shut, trying to remember where he was and how he had gotten there.

It began to come back to him: the fleeting glimpse of someone moving high up among the rocks, the antlers etched against the blue sky, O'Farrell's cry of warning, and the rocks rumbling down. There was that whoosh of dust, blocking out the daylight . . . and then only blackness.

O'Farrell?

The last he remembered, the Irishman was shoving

him out of the way! When he opened his eyes a blinding light from the mouth of the cave drove a needle into his brain. The sun was lower in the sky than he last remembered it. He shut out the pain and wondered how long he had been unconscious. His arms hurt, but when he tried to move them he discovered he couldn't. Something was wrong. A shot of electricity tingled his spine as old instincts took over. His thoughts sharpened and his ears strained to sift the sounds within the cave.

Something was moving about somewhere to his right. A bit of wood struck rock. There was the crackle of a fire. He smelled it too. Something rattled, and then a voice, low and mumbling, reached him. Lying there pretending to be unconscious, Kit listened, trying to make out the words, which at first were strange to his ears. After a moment he began to catch the flow of them.

The voice was that of a woman, and the words she was mumbling were in the Blackfoot tongue. But it was mostly gibberish, a continuous low babble that only half made any sense. That was why it had taken him so long to recognize the language.

Parting an eye, Kit looked without turning his head. His vision wavered in and out of focus at first, still showing the effects of the blow to the head. When it settled he saw the figure hunched over the fire, feeding sticks into the flames. She was dressed in ragged animal skins. Her long black hair was uncombed and adorned with various animal bones. It hung in knots and tangles down her back. She stood and went for more firewood, rattling when she moved, from all the stick, bone, and flashing mica ornamentations fastened about the skins.

She was busy stoking the fire and chattering away to herself in muffled, rambling sentences.

"Sky-eyes, sky-eyes . . . good good."

"Bear-man, Bear-woman, when moon is big. Old Man coming with moon mother."

"Mmmm, Mmmm . . . good, good."

"Sky-eyes, good, hmm."

Kit couldn't make any sense of it. He shifted his view, seeing a bit more of the grotto now, with the low sun slanting deeper into it. The snowshoes had been put back in their place, and lying beside them were his and O'Farrell's rifles. Then something caught his eye. Within her easy reach, she had thrust a wooden staff into a hole in the ground. It stood about five feet tall, and on top of it was the skull of an elk with its spreading antlers reaching nearly to the low ceiling.

Kit turned his attention back to himself and took inventory. He was lying on his side with his arms twisted around behind him. His shoulders burned from the awkward position. For some reason he could not move them. He tested them again and realized why. His wrists had been bound behind his back, and his feet were bound as well. She had tied them in strips of animal hide, with the hair still on it.

Kit twisted his hands in the leather bindings. They gave a little. She had not made the knots tight, and the skin had not been tanned. There was some stretch in them. Kit bunched his fists and began to work at them, feeling the slack grow.

When the woman turned her back to him, he shot a glance at the mouth of the cave. A pile of rocks that had not been there before was scattered around the ledge. But it was O'Farrell Kit was looking for. He did not see the man. Had the avalanche carried him over the edge? If so, then O'Farrell was surely dead. No one could have survived a fall like that.

A high-pitched laugh brought his eyes back around. He narrowed them to a mere sliver as the woman turned and peered hard in his direction. Putting her hands upon hips hidden somewhere deep beneath the layers of rabbit, coyote, and elk skins, she stood there, considering.

Through his slitted eyes, Kit watched her step a little closer. He held still, hardly breathing. In the shadows, it would have been impossible for her to know she was being watched. Just the same, as she drew nearer, he fought back a shrinking feeling that somehow she knew. She stood over him, swaying slightly as if a breeze were blowing through the cave, even though the air was dead still. Then all at once she lifted her bony chin and peered at something behind him.

Kit followed her with his eyes. She stepped past him and bent over something on the floor, just out of his sight.

"Sky-eyes . . . hmm, hmm . . . good, good," she mumbled.

She fussed around behind him for a few minutes, and when she came back around she was carrying a knife. It was O'Farrell's Green River. She dropped to her haunches in front of Kit, running her fingers upon his face. She pinched his cheek two . . . three times as

149

if somehow testing it. Then she parted one of his eye-lids and bent near, peering intently into it.

That so startled him that he almost gave himself away. It was all he could do to keep from staring back at her, or from following her curious gaze.

Her appearance was frightful; she smelled like a wild animal, and her breath held the sting of rotting flesh. When he'd first seen her, he'd judged her to be an old hag. Now he saw that she wasn't. The woman was actually quite young. Curried and scrubbed, she might even have been pretty. But it wasn't her filth that had rattled Kit. It was the ugly scars that covered her face, something no amount of washing and comb-ing could take away. This woman had recently had smallpox—and recovered from it. And not that many months ago.

"Sky-eyes, yes. Mmmm, mmmm . . . good, good," she grunted. Releasing his eyelid, she felt under Kit's heavy coat for the hilt of his butcher knife. She pulled it out and turned it in the sunlight, watching with childlike delight as the bright light glinted off the pol-ished blade and darted along the dark ceiling.

Taking both knives back to the fire, she dropped them into the tattered basket, then fed more wood into the flames and began to sing in a low voice, half hum-ming as she rocked back and forth on her heels.

Sky-eyes? Kit wondered about that a moment. But it wasn't hard to figure it out. She had been looking in his blue eyes when she had said it. O'Farrell had blue eyes too. Now, as he listened, he could hear soft breathing coming from behind him. So the Irishman was still alive, and from the sound of it, unconscious.

Kit considered the rest of what she had said, frowning to himself. It was her *Mmmm, mmmm . . . good, good* that had him particularly nervous. There was little mistaking that sound, or the way she had smacked her lips with anticipation when she had made it.

With a renewed urgency, Kit went back to work on the thongs. He twisted his wrists within them, trying to stretch them enough to slip his hands free, but managing only to gain a fraction of an inch of slack with each passing minute.

While waiting for the flames to burn down into a thick bed of coals—roasting coals, Kit mused unhappily—the woman took up her skull-topped staff and stepped out onto the ledge to peer out over the forest.

While her back was to him and she was otherwise occupied, Kit took the opportunity to swivel his head around. O'Farrell was lying in a heap behind him, out cold. There was so much dried blood on his face, Kit could hardly recognize him. His feet and hands were trussed up with pieces of rawhide, and one of his arms was bent at an unnatural angle. He looked in a bad way. The falling rocks had battered his face to a bloody pulp and had broken at least one bone.

"Sky-eyes, you have come back from your dreamworld."

The voice riveted him. He'd been found out. Kit slowly looked away from O'Farrell. Her glaring, pockmarked face was pinched and frowning as she contemplated him from the ledge. She returned to the cave and stood over him, bent slightly as if unable to fully straighten her spine, holding the staff in one hand.

"Who are you?" he asked in her language.

The woman cocked her head to one side.

"You have a name?"

She listened with great interest, as if the sound of another human voice was something long missing in her life. "I am sister of Coyote," she answered finally. Then, as if surprised to have heard the question in her own language, she added, "*Napi-kwan* speaks the tongue of the People?"

"Yes, I speak the Blackfoot tongue."

Napi-kwan translated roughly to "Old Man Person." Kit had not heard the expression before. He knew the Blackfeet revered a character called "Old Man," who according to legend was the sun, and whose mother was the moon. But "Old Man Person?" This was a new one to him.

"Who is *Napi-kwan*?"

A scowl deepened upon her pocked face and the staff lowered. The sharp tines of the elk antler hovered only inches from his chest. "You *Napi-kwan*. You killer of husbands. You killer of babies!"

"I don't kill babies," he said with a note of indignation. He could not honestly say the same for husbands, and he considered it best to let the matter drop.

"You bring the killer to the People."

That made no sense to him, but before he could wonder what she meant, O'Farrell gave a grunt. Kit and the woman looked over. The Irishman moaned softly and opened his eyes. With the coming of consciousness came O'Farrell's awareness of the suffering he was in. Instantly his face drew into a tight mask of torment from the sharp pain of the broken arm.

"What happened?" he croaked, muddleheaded at first.

"Looks like our trap backfired on us, Sean."

Then O'Farrell saw her. The expression behind the dried blood that caked his face turned from torment to dread and fear. "Saint's, what is it?" he whispered. Talking seemed to hurt him. Kit wondered if one of the falling rocks might not have cracked his jaw as well.

"Thar's your mountain demon, Sean. As it turns out, the demon is a woman. A Blackfoot woman at that, and if I haven't missed my guess, she's got a few loose marbles rattling around inside her think box."

O'Farrell recovered from his shock quickly. "Anyone who would eat a mortified leg has got to have more than just a *few* loose, Mr. Carson."

"Sky-eyes, sky-eyes . . . good, good." The woman stepped around Kit, grasping her staff in both hands as if it were a weapon, one that she knew well how to use. O'Farrell recoiled as it drove toward him, stopping a hairsbreadth from his neck. She laughed at his reaction and wheeled toward Kit, feigning a stab at him too. She did it again and again, just to see him wince. Eventually tiring of the sport, she returned to her fire and poked the flaming brands with a stick, watching the bed of coals growing beneath them.

"What's she up to, Mr. Carson?"

"I can't be sure, but I get the feeling she's planning a feast for tonight. And you or me—one of us—is gonna be the main course."

"Faith! We have to get out of here!" O'Farrell struggled against the leather thongs, only to be stopped by a stab of pain. "My arm is busted," he groaned through pain-clenched teeth. "Can't hardly move,"

The woman looked across at them, scowling.

Kit went back to work on his fetters, but the leather had only so much stretch in it—and not enough for him to slip free. He needed something sharp to saw against. He looked around the cave. There was nothing convenient at hand. Nearby a rock jutted from the dusty floor. That might work . . . if he could get to it. Kit pushed himself up into a sitting position.

The woman grabbed for her antlered staff.

He grinned at her.

When she saw that he just intended to sit there watching, she returned the weapon to its holder and went back to preparing her bed of cooking coals.

As soon as she was again engrossed in her task, Kit slowly scooted backward until the rock pressed up against his heavy coat. The woman commenced to humming to herself, swaying to and fro upon her heels, occasionally glancing up at him. She apparently was so caught up in her own thoughts that she did not seem to be aware of what he was up to. If she had any notion at all, she gave no sign of it.

He smiled disarmingly at her whenever she favored him with one of her curiously blank stares. So as not to arouse her suspicions, he worked on the leather thongs with short, tight movements, slowly sawing them against the rough stone. As he labored at the rock, he glanced around the cave, eyeing their rifles and butcher knives, not seeing their pistols among them. He took comfort in feeling the shape of one of them still in his coat pocket. If only he could have reached it.

"Sky-eyes. Where is my baby?" she asked at one point, glaring at him with a worried scowl.

Kit shook his head. "I don't know."

The woman glanced anxiously about the cave, then went to its mouth and looked outside. She stood upon the ledge, casting about. Then she called for the child. "Little Sparrow! Little Sparrow, come home now."

O'Farrell did not speak the language. "What's she doing now?"

"She's looking for her little one, calling her home."

"Little one? There be no one else here but herself. We'd have seen the tracks if there were two of them."

"I reckon it's part of her condition."

"She's all wasted north of the ears," O'Farrell declared nervously.

"Little Sparrow?" the woman called one last time, peering over the edge at the ground far below. She stepped back inside the cave, scratching her head, and almost at once the thought of the missing child fled her brain. Suddenly she was grinning at nothing in particular that Kit could determine. The woman began singing a lilting tune as she chucked another piece of wood into the fire.

"We've got to get free and out of here," O'Farrell hissed, urgency edging his voice.

"I'm working on it." Kit redoubled his efforts at the stone and felt as if he was gaining ground on the leather straps—though without being able to see them, he couldn't tell how far he had left to go.

"Hurry it up," O'Farrell urged, watching the

woman. "Uh-oh, that she-devil be looking at us sorta funny-like, Mr. Carson."

"Sky-eyes, sky-eyes. Mmmm, mmmm. Yes!" she said suddenly, peering curiously at the two men. A crooked smile slowly spread her pockmarked cheeks and her eyes were wide and purposeful, unlike the vacant stares she had been giving them up until now. She grabbed up one of the knives from the basket and stood.

Giving her lips a lick or two, she said, "Mmm, mmm," and came at them.

"I don't like the looks of this, Mr. Carson," O'Farrell groaned, his eyes stretched wider than an owl's. "She's going to butcher one of us for her dinner, and that's for sure!"

It looked that way to Kit too. "Why don't you put that thar knife down and let's you and me have us a pow-wow," he tried in vain. Nothing ventured, nothing gained. "We got a stash of buffalo meat back to the cabin: hump ribs and tongue. And mighty good eating they are, too. A lot more tasty than a couple stringy mountaineers. Why, this coon is tougher than old boot leather, and O'Farrell thar, he's got more bite to him than an alkali sink."

She was not impressed. Standing there, bucking a nonexistent breeze, considering her choices, she grinned wildly and mumbled over and over, "Sky-eyes. . . . Mmmm, mmmm . . . good, good."

"Mr. Carson," O'Farrell yelped, "she's looking at me like I'm already plucked and stuffed!" His voice shot up to a pitch that no grown man ought to be able to reach.

Kit saw that the demented woman was determined to go through with it, and no amount of jawing was going to deter her. Hands and feet tied up as they were, Kit was practically as helpless as a babe. He had to come up with something, and he had to do it quickly!

Chapter Thirteen

She set her sights upon O'Farrell. What had tipped her one way and not the other, Kit had no way of knowing. Maybe she liked the sound of her own language and wanted to keep him around a little while longer for some friendly jawing before she ate him. Or maybe O'Farrell had a bit more meat on his bones. Or maybe she had no reason at all. Whatever thoughts were rattling around inside her vacant head, they were not of the sort that would make sense to a sane man.

"Mr. Carson!" O'Farrell wailed when she made her move. With his broken arm, he was even more helpless than Kit.

There was no time left to think. Kit rolled away from the rock and, using the only weapon he had left, swung his bound legs in her path, clipping her hard in the shins. She gave a surprised yelp and sprawled across the dusty floor.

Without a second to lose, Kit heaved his legs under himself, rolled over onto his knees, and struggled to his feet. He had to fight gravity and an uneven floor just to keep his balance, swaying there in the center of the cave, unable to move left or right. The woman was quick; she was back on her feet even before he had managed it. She snatched the knife off the floor and, with rage suddenly turning her pocked face into a hideous mask of revenge, let out a wild yell and plunged at him.

Kit had to time it just right. At the last moment he dropped to his haunches and catapulted himself at the deranged woman. His head drove into her midsection like a battering ram, driving her across the cave and hard against the rocky wall. The impact laid Kit out flat and new pain exploded in his neck, along his shoulders, and down into his arms. Momentarily stunned, both combatants didn't move for a moment.

The woman shook her head and staggered away from the wall. She had lost her knife, and she shot a glance at the staff with its deadly rack of antlers.

Kit had no time to get back to his feet. The awkward maneuver would have taken too long and would have exposed his back to her curious and deadly weapon. His legs and feet were all he had to fight with, and he rolled over onto his back and drew his knees into his chest, readying them for her attack.

She grabbed the staff in both hands and wheeled around, snarling like a caged badger. Hunching forward, she leveled the pointed tines at Kit and stalked across the cave. Kit tried his best to keep his feet between the antlers and his chest.

"Sky-eyes . . . baby killer . . . you die now." Aiming for an opening, she thrust it at him.

He managed to deflect the blow, and only barely escaped having a tine run through his foot.

She immediately jogged to her left and tried again. Kit nearly missed it this time. He could not turn fast enough to keep up with her as she danced back to the right. Hard bone slammed into his leg. One of the points ripped open a gash in his buckskin trousers.

Somewhere off to his side he heard O'Farrell shouting, "Watch her now, Mr. Carson. Careful. Don't be giving her no opening now!"

She tried again. He managed to land a foot upon the skull between the antlers, and shoved her back. The blow drove him across the floor several feet and snapped the partly severed thongs binding his wrists. His hands were suddenly free, and he pushed himself up as she lowered the antlers and rushed at him.

Kit threw himself sideways. The tines gouged deep furrows in the dirt floor. She recovered and took aim again. Kit could keep dodging for only so long, and one of these times he was going to be a heartbeat too slow, or miscalculate by a fraction of an inch. And then it would be too late. Locked in the grip of a blinding rage, there could be only one way to stop this woman and end this deadly contest.

It was a last resort, but one she was forcing him to take. Regretting what he had to do, Kit grabbed for the pistol in his coat pocket.

It wasn't there!

A panic momentarily seized him as he searched the pocket in disbelief. Suddenly he realized that what he had felt earlier was not the gun but Andy Bodine's doll! Stunned, he wrapped his fist around it and pulled it out.

The woman was already in a headlong rush, with the wicked points rushing straight for his head and chest, when the doll appeared in Kit's hand.

The sight of it stopped her like a stone wall. Shaking like a leaf in a gale, she stood there staring at the bit of leather and hair, at the cross-stitched eyes and mouth. For a moment, just a brief instant, the insanity left her eyes and cold, sober reality flooded in to take its place. Kit watched the change come over her. Somehow, the doll had triggered a memory, and that memory had jolted her out of her pitiful, foggy existence and brought her face-to-face with sanity.

"Little Sparrow," she cried, staring, her wide eyes brimming. A tear spilled over and drew a streak down her pocked and dirty cheek.

Kit was riveted by the sight of her, the absolute anguish that had instantly replaced the rage. In that moment he saw a torment so crushing fill her miserable soul that he felt it almost as if it had been his own.

"Little Sparrow," she whispered again. Sanity became more than the tortured woman could bear. She let out a wail of despair that shook Kit to the very roots of his soul. Flinging a hand to her mouth, she turned and fled from the cave. As she ran blindly, Kit saw her toe catch on a boulder and she pitched forward. . . .

The wail of her agony followed her all the way down, ending abruptly in that distant, awful muffled thump. Frozen there in shock, Kit stared out of the cave, still not able to believe what he had seen.

161

"Saints!" O'Farrell declared, his voice tempered by awe. "Did you ever see the likes of that?"

Kit shook his head and looked over at the Irishman. The incident had left them both shaken. Finally Kit crawled over to where his knife lay and slit the strips of skin that bound his feet. He cut O'Farrell free, then stepped out onto the ledge. The lowering sun was warm upon his face, and it pushed his shadow clear across the cave and up its back wall. Cautiously, not certain he wanted to see what lay beyond, Kit went to the edge and looked over.

The woman was sprawled in the snow down among the boulders at the base of the cliff. She had landed atop her staff, and Kit could see the tines that had come through her back and had pushed out through her chest. Whatever torment had brought her to this end, it was over now. Grimacing, Kit went back to help O'Farrell.

"Let me see that arm, Sean." Kit felt where the bone had snapped about four inches down from the shoulder.

O'Farrell winced at the pain of his touch and turned his head away. "Is she . . . dead?"

Kit nodded.

"What was all that about . . . what she was saying . . . just before she rushed off?"

"I'm not sure. She said the name of her daughter a couple times, and then something in her brain snapped. I don't know what it meant. But I'll tell you this. Crazy as she might have been, just then, just before she ran off, she was as sane as you or me."

"It was something about that doll. I'd swear to it,"

O'Farrell said. "I saw the way she looked at it when you pulled it from your pocket. What could it have been?"

"I don't know. Don't reckon we'll ever know."

"That was clever of you. How did you know she would take to that wee thing like she did?"

"Clever of me?" Kit laughed. "I thought I was reaching for my gun!"

"Your gun?" Then O'Farrell laughed too.

"Hold tight, this is going to hurt." Kit took a grip on O'Farrell's elbow and pulled back on it until he felt and heard the bone snap into place. O'Farrell ground his teeth and squeezed his eyes, holding back a groan. When it was over, he was near a faint and breathing hard. Kit laid him back on the floor.

"Need to find something to bind it up with for the time being," he said, glancing around. The late sun illuminated the whole cave, and for the first time Kit could see all of it. Where once dark shadows clung, now there was only bare rock wall; where once its depth could only be imagined, now it could be determined with certainty. It was only about fifteen feet deep and maybe twenty wide.

The sunlight picked out the red and blue of a blanket rolled up in a crevice.

"Thar's something that might do."

When he picked up the blanket there was weight to it. He turned back the folds, and the light showed strong upon it. Kit got queasy in the stomach and gave a low groan.

"What's wrong?" O'Farrell asked.

Kit moved aside for him.

"Saints! That be a skeleton?"

Kit gulped down the bile that had climbed to his throat. It was a skeleton. That of a child maybe three or four years old. A little girl, by the scraps of clothing that remained with it. But what had gotten to him was the condition the bones were in. They had been dismembered, and scarred with deep crisscrossing hash marks, as if a knife had been used to strip the flesh from them. All at once Kit understood—understood better than he was comfortable with, and carefully refolded the blanket.

"Little Sparrow wasn't missing after all," he said distantly as a full comprehension of what had happened slowly sank in. "She's been here all the time."

The truth hit O'Farrell like a hammer. "She ate her? She ate her own daughter!" The Irishman's face blanched to the color of powder.

Kit stepped outside for a few minutes where the cold air seemed fresher, and somehow cleaner. This was something Kit had to think about, something that would take some time before he was able to come to grips with it. Something he knew he would never be able to put out of his brain—not completely.

Kit helped Andy Bodine hobble out to where a travois had been slung off the back of his horse and got him settled upon a blanket, making sure he was snug inside his bulky buffalo-skin coat. Upon a second travois, Thomas Conner looked over and managed a grin.

"We're a couple of bookends, we are, you and me, Andy." His voice was still weak, but his spirits were strong. He had come through the ordeal, and that was all that mattered. It had been over a week, and he was still puffing on one lung, but the other was healing, and sounded clear.

"A couple old worn-out bookends," Andy answered. His mood had improved markedly once it was plain that his friend was going to recover. "You and me, we'll have us some dandy yarns to spin around the campfire in the years to come."

Gray Feather lashed Conner to the travois to keep him from being jostled. "You're in fine spirits this morning."

"Just happy to be alive and on my way out of here."

Kit returned to the cabin for the rest of their gear and readied the horses for the trip back to winter quarters. He knew the others would be worried, and probably had already sent out search parties, but the snow had covered their tracks long before. The last week, however, had been gorgeous, with nary a cloud in the sky and temperatures soaring into the fifties. This Rocky Mountain weather was a wonder. One day it would freeze you and the next it would have you down to your shirtsleeves.

Kit checked the cinches on their saddles, then looked around. The snow was wet and heavy, and already vast patches of brown grass were showing on the southern slopes.

"Where did O'Farrell get off to?" he asked. "Just when we're about to pull out of here, he disappears."

Gray Feather gave him a grin and said, "Where do you think? Last I saw of the Irishman, he was headed back thataway." The Ute thrust his jaw at the well-trodden path that climbed the mountain behind the cabin.

"Again?" Kit frowned.

Gray Feather nodded.

"Whal, I better go tell him we're about to leave without him." He grabbed up his rifle and started away, knowing exactly where he would find the Irishman.

The snow around the burial pallet was mostly gone, and the ground soggy. Kit had almost forgotten what it was like to have dry moccasins. Once back at winter quarters, he intended to prop his feet by a fire and not move.

"Saying your last good-byes?" Kit asked.

O'Farrell looked over his shoulder. "You might call it finally burying the dead." His left arm was in a sling, and he held the woman's staff with its crown of antlers in the other.

"You went back for it."

"Thought she'd want to have it, since she never seemed to be without it."

They looked at the burial pallet where now three bodies lay.

"At least they're all together," O'Farrell said. "That should give them some peace."

"You mean so they won't come looking for you?" Kit asked.

He grinned. "Something like that."

"Whal, I wouldn't worry about thar ghosts, O'Farrell. I'm thinking that woman is resting in peace from her earthy ordeal—more peace than she's had for months. I'd say this place is safe from mountain demons."

O'Farrell gave a short laugh, then said seriously,

"You really think it happened like we figured, Mr. Carson?"

Kit shook his head. "Nobody will ever know what happened for sure, but from the looks of it, I'd say so."

"The Blackfeet just left them here? Alone? All three of them because they had the smallpox? That's a hard thing to believe."

"That's the way I put it together. They abandoned them to keep the sickness from spreading. And when her husband died, she buried him like this."

"Reckon the little one died of the pox too?"

Kit grimaced. "I'd prefer to think she did. It's a bitter enough pill to know that a mother could cook and eat a child. I get a little comfort believing the child died first."

O'Farrell shuddered thinking about it and nodded his head. "Aye. That's got to be the way it happened. The poor woman was starvin', she was, and when the little one died, well, she just couldn't help herself. That's the way of it, Mr. Carson I'm sure of it."

"She said I had killed husbands and children. Now I know she didn't mean me personally, but all white men. You and me—everyone. Because it was the white man that had carried the plague to them."

"Aye. And when her hunger forced her to"— O'Farrell couldn't bring himself to say the words— "to do it, why, that must have driven her over the edge."

"Insanity," Kit mused.

"Until she saw Bodine's doll. Something about that doll, about her daughter, snapped her back from her delusions for just a moment."

"And a moment was all it took. The memories were more than she could stand," Kit agreed. "Whal, at least she's at peace now."

They stared at the burial pallet, listening to birds chirping, feeling a warm sun upon their shoulders. Finally Kit said, "Gray Feather and me, we got the horses ready and our passengers loaded onto the travois. We're pulling out, Sean."

O'Farrell carefully placed the staff between the man and his wife, whose arms held the baby. They all had thought it fitting that they should be together like this.

"I'm ready to go. I've buried my ghosts . . . my demon, Mr. Carson."

They turned away from the clearing and, leaving the dead behind, took the living back home.

KIT CARSON

BLOOD RENDEZVOUS
DOUG HAWKINS

The high point of any trapper's year is the summer rendezvous, the annual gathering where mountain men from all over the frontier meet to trade the pelts they risked their lives for. But for Kit Carson, the real danger lies in getting to the rendezvous. He is leading a party of trappers, all of them weighed down with a year's worth of furs. That is enough to make them a tempting target for any killer on the trail—especially when the trail leads through Blackfoot territory.

___4499-4 $3.99 US/$4.99 CAN

KIT CARSON

KEELBOAT CARNAGE
DOUG HAWKINS

The untamed frontier is filled with dangers of all kinds—
both natural and man-made—dangers that only the bravest
can survive. And so far Kit Carson has survived them all.
But when he sets out north along the Missouri River he has
no idea what lies ahead. He can't know that the Blackfeet are
out to turn the river red with blood. And when he hitches a
ride on a riverboat, he can't know that keelboat pirates are
waiting just around the bend!

___4411-0 $3.99 US/$4.99 CAN

KIT CARSON

OREGON TRAVAIL

DOUG HAWKINS

Kit Carson knows trouble could be brewing as he tracks a band of Blackfeet, but he isn't expecting to come upon the remains of a brutal massacre. The Blackfeet butchered a small group of Shoshone, leaving behind nothing but maimed bodies—and one crying baby. Kit sets out to bring the baby back to his people, but the Shoshone find him first. They found the bodies of their families and friends, and have just one thing on their mind—revenge. And with Kit holding the one small survivor of the massacre, he's their only suspect!

___ 4518-6 $3.99 US/$4.99 CAN

Dorchester Publishing Co., Inc.
P.O. Box 6640
Wayne, PA 19087-8640

Please add $1.75 for shipping and handling for the first book and $.50 for each book thereafter. NY, NYC, and PA residents, please add appropriate sales tax. No cash, stamps, or C.O.D.s. All orders shipped within 6 weeks via postal service book rate. Canadian orders require $2.00 extra postage and must be paid in U.S. dollars through a U.S. banking facility.

Name_____

Address_____

City_____ State_____ Zip_____

I have enclosed $_____ in payment for the checked book(s).

Payment **must** accompany all orders. ☐ Please send a free catalog.

CHECK OUT OUR WEBSITE! www.dorchesterpub.com

KIT CARSON

COMANCHE RECKONING

DOUG HAWKINS

There is probably no better tracker in the West than the famous Kit Carson. With his legendary ability to read sign, it is said he can track a mouse over smooth rock. So Kit doesn't expect any trouble when he sets out on the trail of a common thief. But he hasn't counted on a fierce blizzard that seems determined to freeze his bones. Or on a band of furious Comanches led by an old enemy of Kit's—an enemy dead set on revenge.

___4453-6 $3.99 US/$4.99 CAN

WILDERNESS

#27
GOLD RAGE
DAVID THOMPSON

Penniless old trapper Ben Frazier is just about ready to pack it all in when an Arapaho warrior takes pity on him and shows him where to find the elusive gold that white men value so greatly. His problems seem to be over, but then another band of trappers finds out about the gold and forces Ben to lead them to it. It's up to Zach King to save the old man, but can he survive a fight against a gang of gold-crazed mountain men?

___4519-2 $3.99 US/$4.99 CAN

Dorchester Publishing Co., Inc.
P.O. Box 6640
Wayne, PA 19087-8640

Please add $1.75 for shipping and handling for the first book and $.50 for each book thereafter. NY, NYC, and PA residents, please add appropriate sales tax. No cash, stamps, or C.O.D.s. All orders shipped within 6 weeks via postal service book rate. Canadian orders require $2.00 extra postage and must be paid in U.S. dollars through a U.S. banking facility.

Name_____
Address_____
City_____ State_____ Zip_____
I have enclosed $_____ in payment for the checked book(s).
Payment <u>must</u> accompany all orders. ❏ Please send a free catalog.
CHECK OUT OUR WEBSITE! www.dorchesterpub.com

WILDERNESS

BLOOD FEUD

◄━━━━━━━━━━━━━━━━━►

David Thompson

The brutal wilderness of the Rocky Mountains can be deadly to those unaccustomed to its dangers. So when a clan of travelers from the hill country back East arrive at Nate King's part of the mountain, Nate is more than willing to lend a hand and show them some hospitality. He has no way of knowing that this clan is used to fighting—and killing—for what they want. And they want Nate's land for their own!
___4477-3 $3.99 US/$4.99 CAN

WILDERNESS

#25
FRONTIER MAYHEM

←——————————→

David Thompson

The unforgiving wilderness of the Rocky Mountains forces a boy to grow up fast, so Nate King taught his son, Zach, how to survive the constant hazards and hardships—and he taught him well. With an Indian war party on the prowl and a marauding grizzly on the loose, young Zach is about to face the test of his life, with no room for failure. But there is one danger Nate hasn't prepared Zach for—a beautiful girl with blue eyes.

___4433-1 $3.99 US/$4.99 CAN

Dorchester Publishing Co., Inc.
P.O. Box 6640
Wayne, PA 19087-8640

Please add $1.75 for shipping and handling for the first book and $.50 for each book thereafter. NY, NYC, and PA residents, please add appropriate sales tax. No cash, stamps, or C.O.D.s. All orders shipped within 6 weeks via postal service book rate. Canadian orders require $2.00 extra postage and must be paid in U.S. dollars through a U.S. banking facility.

Name_____
Address_____
City_____ State_____ Zip_____
I have enclosed $_____ in payment for the checked book(s).
Payment <u>must</u> accompany all orders. ❑ Please send a free catalog.
CHECK OUT OUR WEBSITE! www.dorchesterpub.com